Game Play

LISA SUZANNE

GAME PLAY
VEGAS ACES: THE COACH
BOOK THREE
© LISA SUZANNE 2023

All rights reserved. In accordance with the US Copyright Act of 1976, the scanning, uploading, and sharing of any part of this book without the permission of the publisher or author constitute unlawful piracy and theft of the author's intellectual property. No part of this book may be reproduced or transmitted in any form or by any means, electronic or mechanical, including photocopying, recording, or by any information storage and retrieval system without the written permission of the author, except where permitted by law and except for excerpts used in reviews. If you would like to use any words from this book other than for review purposes, prior written permission must be obtained from the publisher.

Published in the United States of America by Books by LS, LLC.

ISBN: 9798870197883

This book is a work of fiction. Any similarities to real people, living or dead, is purely coincidental. All characters and events in this work are figments of the author's imagination.

Vegas Aces The Coach: Game Play

Books by Lisa Suzanne

VEGAS ACES
Home Game (Book One)
Long Game (Book Two)
Fair Game (Book Three)
Waiting Game (Book Four)
End Game (Book Five)

VEGAS ACES: THE QUARTERBACK
Traded (Book One)
Tackled (Book Two)
Timeout (Book Three)
Turnover (Book Four)
Touchdown (Book Five)

VEGAS ACES: THE TIGHT END
Tight Spot (Book One)
Tight Hold (Book Two)
Tight Fit (Book Three)
Tight Laced (Book Four)
Tight End (Book Five)

VEGAS ACES: THE WIDE RECEIVER
Rookie Mistake (Book One)
Hidden Mistake (Book Two)
Honest Mistake (Book Three)
No Mistake (Book Four)
Favorite Mistake (Book Five)

VEGAS ACES: THE PLAYBOOK
Fumbled (Book 1)
False Start (Book 2)
Fair Catch (Book 3)
Forward Progress (Book 4)
Field Goal (Book 5)

Visit Lisa on Amazon for more titles

Dedication

To my 3Ms.

CHAPTER 1

Jolene

I skid to a stop in Jeremy's driveway and I ring the bell before I start banging on the door.

I sort of wish Lincoln was with me.

I don't like going into this alone, but I'm here to protect Jonah, and there is nothing I wouldn't do for him.

The door opens, and Jeremy is red-faced and clearly angry. Alyssa is on her hands and knees behind him with a dustpan sweeping shards of something onto it.

"I'm here for Jonah," I say point blank.

"Excuse me?" he thunders at me. "It's my weekend!" Even from the short distance between us, I can smell the yeast of too much beer and cigarette smoke on him.

"Yeah, but when your kid calls you for pickup because he can't sleep over all the fighting, you rush right over." I keep my voice calm and matter of fact even though I'm ready to go postal on this idiot.

"Then call a goddamn lawyer," he hisses, and he slams the door in my face.

Oh fuck that. Fuck him. Fuck this entire fucking night.

I start banging on the door again, and I don't stop even when my fists are screaming in pain. I'm not leaving without Jonah.

A few moments pass before Alyssa opens the door. Her face is streaked with tears, but Jeremy isn't around. My best guess is that he went to pass out from whatever he did tonight.

"I'll go get him for you," she says softly.

"What's going on?" I ask as she waves me into the house.

"Jeremy went out with his friends from work and came home drunk," she says, her voice low and devoid of emotion as we walk through the house toward Jonah's room. "We got into it because he stayed out hours later than he said he would. He doesn't usually drink like this, not when Jonah's here anyway, but they were celebrating a new product they're launching soon, and I guess he had more than he should have."

"Are you okay?" I ask quietly.

We're not friends. She slept with Jeremy when I was pregnant with Jonah, after all. But I will always side with a woman who is in danger, even when she's the homewrecker who broke us up.

She did me a favor. I realize that now—but she doesn't deserve any of this. No one does.

She starts crying again, but she nods as we stop outside the hallway toward the kids' rooms. I can hear one of the little girls crying in her room, but I'm not sure which bedroom it's coming from. "I'm not in any danger. He'll sleep it off and everything will be back to normal tomorrow."

"Does this happen often?" I ask.

She shrugs and wipes away a tear without answering.

GAME PLAY

"If you need somewhere to go…" I trail off and let that hang between us. I can't exactly invite her to Sam's place. I'm already in the guest room, and the boys are sharing a room.

But if we have to make room for her safety, we will.

"It's fine. I appreciate that, but me and the girls…we're okay."

I nod. "If you're sure."

She presses her lips together, and she glances toward the opposite side of the house. "Yeah. I'm sure."

"Okay." I walk up to Jonah's door and knock softly. "Jonah? It's me."

The door opens, and he rushes into my waist, wrapping his arms around me. I lean down to hold him against me, and that heaviness in my chest only seems to worsen as he starts to cry.

"I'm going to take him home now," I tell Alyssa.

She nods. "I'm so sorry, Jonah." She ruffles his hair a little. "You deserve better."

"Thanks, Lyss," he says, and he gives her a quick hug before I usher him toward the front door.

"Call me if you need anything," I tell Alyssa, and she mouths a *thank you* before she closes the door behind us and presumably heads toward the bedroom with her two crying girls.

Jonah heaves out a heavy sigh once he's buckled into Cade's booster in the back. "Why do you have Sam's car?" he asks.

"Oh, uh…" I scramble to come up with a reason, and I feel terrible for lying to him. He's been through enough tonight. He deserves an honest answer, but I can't exactly tell him I'm sleeping with Lincoln Nash, the son of his grandfather's mortal enemy. "It's a long story." I leave it at that. "Are you okay?"

"Yeah. Just tired."

"Well tomorrow's Sunday, and you can sleep in as late as you want. We'll go to Grammy and Pop-Pop's for pancakes and bacon whenever you get up. Sound good?" I make a mental note to ask my parents if we can come over for breakfast, but they make bacon every Sunday, and it's a standing invitation.

"Yeah," he says, his voice subdued, and my heart breaks that his father is the one who did this to him.

As soon as I get home, I'm emailing my lawyer so I can figure out how to change this custody agreement. I hate that Jeremy has this effect on my child, and if I can stop it from happening again, I will.

He's exhausted by the time we get home, and the house is quiet. Sam's asleep, and I assume she figured I wouldn't be coming home tonight.

I usher him into the house and tuck him into bed. I pepper his cheeks with a million kisses before I head toward the kitchen and leave a note for Sam on the counter so she isn't scared when she wakes up to find us both here.

And then I head toward my bedroom, ready to slip out of my clothes and into my pajamas so I can put this awful night in the past.

But when I flick on my light, I see the outline of a figure lying on my bed. I jump about a thousand feet into the air, my heart racing all the way up to my throat, and I'm about to scream when he waves at me and my brain catches up to the fear.

"Oh my God, you scared the shit out of me!" I whisper-yell.

GAME PLAY

Lincoln chuckles a bit. "I'm sorry. I know it's been a tough night on you, and I didn't want you to be alone."

"But your car isn't here—"

He shakes his head. "I took a Lyft over. What happened?"

Just as I finish relaying the story, my phone dings with a new text.

What now?

I heave out a breath as I check the message.

Rivera: *So strange that Sam went to your kid's dad's place tonight and left with your kid. Or is it that you're driving your friend's car around now to avoid getting caught coming and going from the Coach's place? [shrug emoji]*

"Fuck," I mutter.

"What now?" he asks, voicing the exact thought in my own head from a second ago.

I toss the phone to him while I change into my pajamas.

"This guy is a real fucking thorn," he says.

I purse my lips as I slide into bed beside him, and I take my phone and set it on the nightstand beside me. I turn back toward him and snuggle onto his chest as he loops an arm around my shoulders. "What are we going to do? He wants my job, and he's not going to stop until he gets it."

"Can you talk to your boss? Or maybe someone at HR?" he suggests. He presses his lips to the top of my head.

"What good will it do?" I ask. "Then he'll just have a bigger vendetta against me."

"Maybe they'd have additional suggestions for you. Maybe he can be transferred to a different department. He could cover a different team. I don't know." He's throwing out suggestions, but they're all things I've already thought about.

"He's an expert in football. He wanted *this* position."

"What about at another channel? What if you get him ousted at VG-oh-three but he's let go quietly and recommended elsewhere?" he suggests. "Could be a great new opportunity for him."

"Nobody has openings right now, so he's picking at the most vulnerable thread."

"You? Vulnerable?" He shakes his head. "Nope. You're smart, confident, and badass. You will find a way to take him down."

I wish I was as sure about that as he is.

CHAPTER 2

Jolene

Despite the shitshow that was my Saturday night, somehow I sleep better than I have since...Ohio.

Sleeping next to Lincoln calms me in a way I didn't know I could be calmed.

But waking up in his arms...that's a different story entirely. My kid is in the next room, and even though I *said* he could sleep in, he still won't sleep past eight. And more than likely, he'll come into my room if I'm still in bed.

And so I pop up out of bed the second I wake. I check my phone and see it's a little before eight, and I reach over and shake Lincoln awake.

"Dude, you gotta go," I shout in a whisper. "Jonah's gonna wake up any second and you can't be here when he does."

"Just five more minutes," he mutters, rolling over and pulling the pillow over his head.

"Lincoln!" I'm still shouting but in a soft voice. "Wake the fuck up!"

I'm starting to get a little frantic, which is silly, but I don't want my child to catch whatever this is before we get to define what it is.

"Can't I just go out to the couch and we'll tell him I'm here with Samantha?" he suggests.

It's actually…not a terrible idea for this early in the morning after a late night where we talked and I cried and we only got about five hours of solid sleep.

"Fine, but you have to get out of here."

"Okay, okay," he mutters, and he forces himself up. He grabs his clothes and starts getting dressed. Slowly.

"Out!" I whisper, pointing at the door.

"Sorry!" he whisper yells back, and it would be comical if I wasn't panicking to get him out of here.

He glances out into the hallway, sees the coast is clear, and blows me a kiss before he closes the door behind himself.

Whew. That was close.

I take a minute to soak in that kiss he blew me, and then I rush into the bathroom to grab a quick shower. I look in the mirror and see the giant bags under my eyes—a byproduct of crying before I fell asleep, and I look like hell warmed over.

The shower helps a little, but I still feel on edge. Between Rivera's threats, whatever's going on with Jeremy, and Lincoln being here when Jonah is also here, there's just too many things that can go wrong. I still need to email my lawyer, and I tie my wet hair into a bun and grab my laptop to take it out to the kitchen to try to beat Jonah out there when I hear voices in the family room.

Shit.

I didn't beat Jonah out there after all.

GAME PLAY

I pull myself together. Fake it 'til you make it, Bailey.

I stop short when I see the two of them sitting on the couch.

Jonah is smiling. *Smiling*. And laughing! As if I didn't have to go get him from his dad's house last night because he was terrified. You always hear people say kids are resilient, and maybe they are. I still think it depends on an awful lot of things, and that saying is just something people made up to make themselves feel better about the trauma kids sometimes face. But in this situation...Jonah really seems to have bounced right back.

He's happy.

And Lincoln is smiling, too. I have no idea why. I glance at the television screen and see they're watching some movie with those little yellow minion guys, and I can't honestly imagine Lincoln Fucking Nash sitting down to the *Minions* movie...yet here he is, laughing with Jonah over some inside joke they'll get to share now, and I'm on the outside and oddly somehow perfectly okay with it when the *last* thing I should be is okay with this *enemy* of mine having a moment with my little boy.

"Good morning, kiddo," I say to Jonah, and I essentially ignore Lincoln even though seeing him laughing with my kid on the couch does something to me.

Something terrifying.

Something that feels like forever when I already know we can't possibly *have* forever.

I walk over and plant a kiss on top of Jonah's head, and I'm close enough that Lincoln runs a flirty finger along my thigh without Jonah seeing.

The thought of what those fingers have the power to do to me makes me shiver, and I give him a glare.

Merriment is still in his eyes as he catches my glare, and I can't help when the glare turns to a slight giggle.

Sam emerges from the hallway rather bleary-eyed, and she freezes when she spots the three of us in her family room. Clearly she just woke up, and even more evident is the fact that she hasn't seen my note yet.

"Oh, uh…there you are," she says sort of half-heartedly to Lincoln.

"Hey babe," he calls from the couch.

And I might be hearing things, but I *swear* I hear Jonah mutter, "I wish you were dating my mom."

I run from the room toward the kitchen before I say something I shouldn't.

But it's clear from the laughing in there that my son is now involved in this mess, and I don't like that one little, tiny bit.

I take a quick moment to compose an email to my lawyer detailing to her what happened last night so it's on record, and then I end the email by telling her I no longer think it's safe for Jonah to go to his dad's every other weekend. I click send and hope for the best.

"Jonah, can you get dressed, bud?" I yell from the kitchen as Sam walks toward me.

"I wanna stay with Lincoln!" he calls back.

"There's pancakes and bacon in it for you!"

I hear the low rumble of Lincoln saying something to my son.

"Ugh! Fine!" he moans, and then I hear him run down the hallway to his room.

"I take it you let Lincoln in last night?" I say to Sam.

She nods. "Is Jonah okay?"

GAME PLAY

"Yeah, he's okay. I guess Jeremy came home drunk and he and Alyssa got into it. Jonah was scared and called me to come get him."

"What does *got into it* mean?" she asks, clearly alarmed.

"It means Alyssa was cleaning up what appeared to be shards of broken glass when I arrived."

"Jesus," she mutters. "You okay?"

"I will be when I hear back from my lawyer confirming that I don't need to continue sending him over there. I can't do it, Sam. It's awful."

"And after our fight at the event last night...just shit piled on top of more shit," she says.

I twist my lips. "More than you know." I'm referring to Rivera, which I still haven't mentioned to her, but I can't when Jonah is only seconds from hopping down the hall so we can go to breakfast.

I text my mom to let her know we're coming over, and Sam is giving me a curious glance.

"What's more than I know?" she asks.

"I'll tell you later." I scramble out of the kitchen toward Jonah's doorway. "Brush your teeth, kiddo. Then we'll go, okay?"

"Can't I hang out with Coach Nash a little longer?" he begs.

"Sorry, bud. I'm sure Mr. Nash has things to do today, and my tummy is rumbling."

"Fine," he mutters, and he heads to the bathroom to brush his teeth.

When I walk back into the kitchen, Lincoln is waiting around the corner, and he grabs me to steal a quick kiss.

I can't help a breathless laugh when he lets me go. "Have a good day," I say softly.

"I don't know about that," he says quietly.

"How come?"

"I got to wake up next to you and now I'm leaving you. It all goes downhill from here."

I make a sad face at him, but his words hit me straight in the chest.

I don't know how we're going to keep up this ruse—especially not if my son is going to be here every night.

But I damn well know I'm going to move heaven and Earth to figure out how.

CHAPTER 3

Jolene

"Jonah-Bear!" my mom says when she opens the door, and I feel the *instant* guilt that I woke up in Lincoln Nash's arms as I walk into my parents' house. My mom pulls my boy into her arms, and my dad is right behind her with a hug for me.

I wonder if I still smell like his cologne.

My dad gives me a curious glance as he pulls away, and I'm certain he can tell something's up.

That instant guilt turns into a flood.

What Lincoln and I are doing goes against everything we were both brought up separately to believe. If there's one thing our parents would agree on, it's that loyalty to family comes first. And we're both breaking that law right now.

The rest of the morning only proves that to be true.

We sit down to breakfast, and Jonah brings it up. "Guess who was at my house this morning!"

My dad looks at him and grins. "Hm…was it one of those creeper guys from your game?"

"Nope!" Jonah says gleefully.

"Was it Cade?" my mom asks.

"Wrong again!" he says as he takes a bite of bacon.

"Who?" they ask him at the same time, and my chest squeezes as he says the name.

"Coach Nash, the new coach for the Aces!" he cries out. "He is *so* cool. He watched *Minions* with me!"

"Nash?" my dad says. "Really?" He turns toward me. "You're letting your kid hang out with Nash?"

I feel…exposed. Seen. Nervous. Is this it?

"He's going out with Cade's mom," Jonah explains.

Phew.

At least I'm not the one who's responsible for relaying that information to my parents.

"With Sam?" my mom says, her eyes turning toward me. "And how do *you* feel about that?"

I shrug. "We sort of got into an argument about it last night," I admit, though I don't want to be having this conversation in front of my son who basically idolizes the man.

"You and Sam did?" my mom clarifies.

I clear my throat. "Yes. She knows how we feel."

"About what?" Jonah asks.

"About that good for nothing Nash family," my dad mutters. "You know his dad purposely hurt me during practice so badly that I never got to play football again?"

"We don't know that, Dad," I say, immediately jumping to the Nash's defense—which I realize too late is great for my son but horrible for my parents.

My mom gasps at my outburst, and my father turns hard eyes on me. "First he took me out of the game, and then he tried to oust me from my own business." He shakes his head. "And he used his sons against us, too. He tried to get them involved in the fight, and that family fights dirty. I wouldn't

GAME PLAY

put it past that coach to use your friend to try to manipulate you." He's talking to me, and I'm looking at my son, who looks like he just lost a hero.

I'm devastated for him, and I have no idea what to say.

I really didn't think Lincoln would be the focus of our entire breakfast, but clearly I was mistaken. I barely even touch my bacon, my appetite suddenly gone.

I wait until later when we're on our way home to talk to my son about what happened. I can't seem to do it in front of my dad, and I hate that I still feel that pressure after all these years.

But it is, after all, a big reason why Lincoln and I have to be careful.

"Honey, it's okay if you like Mr. Nash."

I glance at him in my rearview mirror. He's looking out the window and he doesn't say anything, and it breaks my heart. After last night…it just feels like the kid has been through enough.

"Grampy just doesn't like his dad."

"But he said the dad got the sons involved—" he starts, but I interrupt.

"And I want *you* to form your own opinion of him." I say it firmly and clearly even though I obviously haven't allowed myself to take the same advice.

"Then how come you hate him?" he asks.

"I don't hate him," I protest. "I was just raised to stay far away from him, I guess." I don't really know how else to explain it to him—or how to explain why it's okay for him to like him but not me. So instead, I say, "I don't want to do that to you, baby. I don't think it's fair."

"Okay," he mumbles, but I get the feeling he doesn't really buy into what I'm selling him.

21

Lincoln is gone when we get back home, and I assume he left shortly after we did.

And it's as we finish the *Minions* movie that I realize I never replied to Rivera's text last night. Instead of giving him the satisfaction, I ignore him.

It feels safer that way.

But that feeling of safety is just an illusion because Monday morning rolls around again, and I make it to the conference room for our meeting first.

Rivera makes it in second.

I don't want to be alone with him, yet here we are.

"You never responded to my text," he says quietly.

"You pinned me up against a wall and very nearly assaulted me," I retort. "I don't feel like I owe you a damn thing."

He presses his lips together and shakes his head a little. "Oh come on, Bailey. Assault? Hardly."

"Says every predator ever."

"Predator?" he repeats. "Now you're just grasping at straws."

"Am I? Or did you cross a line you shouldn't have?"

He doesn't look nervous by my tone even though he should. Instead, he issues more threats. "What are you going to do about it? Because I still have those pictures, and I'm not afraid to use them."

"Go ahead," I say flippantly, calling his bluff.

He looks surprised by my words. "I'll get them to Marcus today, then."

"Okay. Go ahead. And I'll march straight up to HR to let them know how you're stalking me, taking photos of me without my consent, and had me pinned up against a wall while hitting on me at a professional event."

GAME PLAY

"Your word against mine," he says smugly.

I stare at him pointedly even though just the sight of him is making my skin crawl and my stomach knot up.

The door opens and Sanders walks in with Marcus, effectively ending our conversation as the room fills with the rest of our sports staff.

The meeting gets underway, but I don't miss the dirty looks Rivera continues to shoot in my direction.

God, I hate that fucker. But two can play his little game, and if he's going to continue to threaten to expose the pictures of Lincoln and me, well, I have shit on him, too, including a screenshot of the text he sent me last night.

He's not as smart as he thinks he is, and I'm not about to let him win this little game.

Marcus hands out our assignments, and when the meeting is over, he asks me to stay behind.

Rivera raises his brows as if to say this only confirms that I'm sleeping with Marcus, which…whatever. I can't change his mind about that any more than I can every other person who thinks it regardless of whether it's true. Marcus is married and has four kids. He's a dedicated family man, and he wouldn't stray on his wife, but none of that enters the discussion when we're discussing women in sports reporting.

Once the room clears, Marcus shuts the door and perches on the edge of the table. He folds his hands together in front of him and turns toward me. "Talk to me about that very public fight on Saturday at the team event."

I clear my throat.

Maybe I should just tell him. I really believe he's someone I can trust, and telling him might help me get ahead of any potential issues with Rivera.

And so I make a snap decision, praying it's the right one.

I clear my throat. "Lincoln Nash and I...we have a history."

"A history," he repeats.

I nod. "You know the stuff about our dads, but Lincoln and I...we were best friends, too. We did everything together, and friendship became more along the way. And then he ended things with me right after his father took my father out."

His brows push together. "Definitely related."

"Never confirmed, but more than likely. My family moved. We lost touch, and now he's here in *my* town again. We fought it as long as we could, but..."

"Oh shit," he mutters, and he closes his eyes as he pinches the bridge of his nose. "Please don't tell me."

"This stays between us." I'm trying not to beg here.

"Always."

I sigh. "This thing with my friend—it's a ruse to throw the shade off what we're doing."

"Which is?"

"Hiding as we try to figure it out."

"Shit, Jolene," he mutters, and of all the things I was expecting out of him, it wasn't for him to be mad at me. But I also guess that speaks to how well we've been hiding it. For now. "You're putting your career—your *family*—at risk, and for what?"

"I don't know," I say as I shrug. "But what we have...it's strong, Marcus. It's powerful. It's once in a lifetime."

"Fuckin' better be if you're willing to throw everything on the line."

"I'm not throwing anything on the line," I protest.

GAME PLAY

"His dad is rumored to have purposely hurt your dad. Why do you think he might've done that?" he asks.

"It's the great mystery of my life. It's so much easier for me to believe he didn't intend to hurt him, that it was purely an accident."

"There was no reason for him to pull that move on your father," he says. "So dig a little deeper, correspondent."

I shake my head. "What good would it do?"

"For one, it would show your true colors. Are you an unbiased sports reporter? Or are you letting your emotions cloud the stories you need to tell this season because you're carrying on with the coach?"

His words rile me right up. I stand and place my palms on the table. "I got this job before we knew he'd be the head coach, and I will continue to report the way I always have on this team."

"And if you run into something that might upset your boyfriend?" he presses, and I *know* he's only asking so he can get a rise out of me and see me maintain my cool. It's a test.

"If it needs to be made public, I assure you, it will be."

"Right, then. Carry on."

"One more thing," I say.

He raises his brows.

"Rivera got pictures of Lincoln and me."

"Doing what?" he snaps.

"Kissing." I glance down at the table rather than meeting his judgmental eyes.

"Jesus, already?"

"And he's been threatening me with them. Among other things." I feel like a child telling on the schoolyard bully.

"What things?" he asks.

"I plead the fifth. I just wanted you to know photos exist."

"When did he get them?"

"End of March."

"Well over two months ago? And he hasn't used them yet?" he asks.

"I think he gets off on using them to threaten me," I admit. "I don't want him to know you know. Let me handle it."

He nods. "Fine. But I'll keep an eye on him. Just be careful, Jolene. I mean it."

I nod. "I will."

He lets out a heavy sigh before he walks out of the room, and I'm not sure whether it was a smart move or a dumb one to admit what's been going on.

I guess there's no turning back now.

CHAPTER 4

lincoln

"Yes, yes, yes!" she whispers.

She has to whisper. She's in my office, her legs in the air and her back on the little round table in the corner as I bang into her. I wish I'd had the foresight to take her out of her dress so I could watch her tits bounce, but we scrambled to get to this moment as it is.

"Fuck," I murmur as I come into her. It's a long, hard climax a couple weeks in the making, and I drop down to press my lips to hers as my body wrings itself out into her.

We've barely had time for each other, but there was a press conference earlier and she asked me for an exclusive afterward, so here we are.

She's definitely getting exclusive treatment.

I straighten to brush my fingertips along her clit after my body stops pulsing into hers, but I don't pull out quite yet.

And that sends her straight into the orgasm *she* needs, too.

God, it's fucking hot to watch her face as she comes.

Her eyelids are heavy as she moans my name, and she snags her bottom lip between her teeth as the climax plows into her. Her legs wrap around my midsection as I continue to fuck her slowly, and her back arches off the table as she comes.

She lets out a soft little sigh when it's all over, and eventually I have to pull out of her. I slide her panties back up her legs.

"Always happy to share an exclusive with you, Ms. Bailey," I say with a wink, and she giggles as she pulls her clothes back into place.

"I really should probably ask you a few questions. Are you ready for the rest of this week's OTAs?"

I grab a tissue to clean off my dick and head to my private bathroom while we talk. "I'm ready. I can't wait to get a feel for the energy and vibe this team will have going into our new season."

"What are you going to do with your four hours Thursday and Friday?" she asks.

"Well, I finally get to be out there with my players again, so we'll run some drills and start getting a feel for how each position works together." I emerge from the bathroom and perch on the edge of my desk.

She asks me a few more questions for good measure, things that weren't already covered in the press conference, and then she eyes me a little nervously.

"What?" I ask.

She clears her throat. "I need to tell you something."

I narrow my eyes at her. "What?" I repeat.

"I, um…I told Marcus about us."

My chest tightens for a beat. One more person knows. That's one more person capable to outing us. "You…what? I thought we agreed nobody except Sam."

GAME PLAY

"We did, but with the threats coming in from Rivera...I don't know." She shakes her head as her eyes fall toward the ground. "Marcus pulled me aside on Monday to ask me about the fight over the weekend. I came clean and told him about Rivera."

"Everything about Rivera?"

"No."

I sigh. "Okay. We can trust him?"

"We can trust him," she confirms.

"If you say so."

"Are you mad?" she asks. She glances up at me with a bit of fear, and I don't like that she feels nervous to hear my reaction.

"No, I'm not mad. I'm just surprised."

"He told me to be careful."

I nod. "We will." I move toward her and take her in my arms again. "It's our only choice."

And it's not hard to be careful when we barely get the chance to see one another. Over the next couple weeks, I really only see her at one OTA practice each week, and it's like a goddamn beam of sunshine bursting from a raincloud the moment I spot her.

This week was our voluntary minicamp. It's Friday night before the big charity ball that I'm honorary chair of—something that's taken up very little of my time, to be honest, but at least I know tomorrow I'll get to see her even though I'm attending with her best friend.

And she's been busy with her kid. Her lawyer informed her that in order to change the visitation rights with her ex, she has to file a motion with the court proving he's unfit to be with their son. So she's been fighting for her son while

I've been working, and unfortunately we haven't had much time to connect.

I don't acknowledge her at practice. I can't. She's with the media, and I have my own work to do. We're installing new plays, practicing without contact, going through the motions. There's a lot to break down here, and I'm using every second I can on the field to make sure my team will be ready for camp next month. We're limited in what we can do thanks to the player's association—which is great to keep players safe, but it also puts in place restrictions on both time and the sorts of activities we can have players participate in.

Still, knowing she's there watching this gives me a different sort of perspective that I like more than I'm willing to admit. She gets it. She's not harping on why we never get to see each other. Instead, she has a life of her own, one that coincides with the things I'm doing, and as I think toward a future with her, I can't help but think that's one more thing that sets her apart from anyone else I've ever been with. She gets me. She gets my schedule. She grew up in this life, and she's a part of it now, too.

It's refreshing. It's also scary as fuck since the chances of us actually achieving that future are slim.

OTAs are voluntary for players, but the majority of the team shows up because these are fucking football players. They're here because they love the game. Guys don't make it to this league if they aren't serious about it, and we're all putting in the work that comes with a new coach.

Some of our rookies are excelling, showing us what they're made of, and I'm excited to see more of it in training camp next month. It's the real start of the season for us even though we have these shorter sessions, and I'm ready for it to get underway. The anticipation is killing me already.

GAME PLAY

I should have plenty to do on a Friday night, but I'm beat to hell after minicamp this week. Three full days this week with players showing what they're made of, and with me being present for every fucking second.

It was both exhilarating and exhausting.

Jack invited me out for a few drinks to celebrate the week and recap, but I declined. We recapped a bit this morning at the office, and we can recap more Monday. It was a long week, and I need a night away before I gear up to take my girl's best friend to a charity ball tomorrow.

So imagine my surprise when a text comes through a little after six and I happen to be home.

Lorraine: *Just dropped J off at my parents' for a double sleepover. Maybe we can have one too?*

I chuckle as I read her text.

We haven't had a sleepover since the night she picked up Jonah from his dad's house and I snuck over to spend the night with her in my arms.

It's been far too long, that's for damn sure.

Me: *I am ALL IN. Get that sweet little ass of yours over here NOW.*

She sends me the red face panting emoji, and I chuckle at my phone.

And then I wait.

CHAPTER 5

Jolene

I park Sam's car in Lincoln's driveaway, carefully checking the rearview mirror to be sure nobody followed me over this time.

I think I'm safe, but I still wear my hood up over my hair as I rush to his front door.

Last time I was here, I was so shaken by what went down with Rivera and then I got called away early to get my son, so I didn't really get to explore the abode belonging to Mr. Lincoln Nash.

A person's home can tell you an awful lot about a guy, but I didn't get the chance to learn much of anything last time.

This time, I'm taking my time. I want the grand tour, and I want him to make love to me in every single room so when he walks into each one, he thinks of me and what we did in there.

Okay, maybe that's too much too soon.

We'll see if I get up the nerve to actually say that to him.

He opens the door before I ring the bell, and he's standing there in jeans, a black shirt, and no socks or shoes.

He's just home on a Friday night all casual and hot with that scruff lining his jaw and those dark eyes of his hot on mine, and I'm not sure how I got so lucky.

Or maybe it's not luck at all. What we have is simply a curse since I'm madly in love with him yet can't really be with him the way normal couples can be.

What a confusing hot mess.

"Hi," I say tentatively once the door is shut behind me.

"Hey. Come on in."

I'm carrying a duffel bag, and he takes it from me and sets it on the floor by the stairs to go up whenever we do.

I follow him toward his kitchen, a room I never got to explore the last time I was here. It has white quartz countertops and a subway tile backsplash with black cabinets and a white floor. It's all black and white, very monochrome, but something about it is both sexy and alluring.

"Are you hungry? I was just going to order some takeout."

"What if we make dinner instead?" I ask.

"Make dinner?" he echoes.

"Yeah…like cook? You know, how normal people make food and then eat it?"

"Are you saying I'm not normal?" he counters.

I laugh. "No, but cooking can be both relaxing and therapeutic."

"So is getting a massage, but there's no dishes to clean up afterward."

"Ha, ha, smart guy. Do you keep anything around here or do you order all your meals?" I ask, curious about his actual lifestyle.

"I have some stuff around." He nods toward the fridge and his pantry. "Feel free to take a peek around."

GAME PLAY

I chuckle but start my exploration, and I find enough stuff to be able to make breakfast for dinner. As I'm bending down to check the bottom shelf of his rather large pantry, I feel his hand connect with my ass, a rather loud *crack* filling the pantry.

"Hey!" I protest, rubbing my ass.

"You can't really expect me not to touch your ass when you're presenting it to me like that."

I shoot him a glare. "Turnabout's fair play, my friend. If I see your ass up in the air, I'm smacking it, too."

"Deal. As long as I get to touch your ass, I'm a happy man."

I giggle. "Right. So…scrambled eggs, toast, and sausage?"

"I've got the sausage covered," he says, and he grabs his groin.

I roll my eyes. "Already with the sausage jokes," I mutter.

"What?" he protests. "Sausage jokes and slapping your ass any time you bend over. It's like a *staple* of making a dinner together, isn't it?"

"Is it, though? Does it *have* to be?"

He laughs, and we get started cooking a meal together. He doesn't know his way around the kitchen very well, which tells me he's used to ordering takeout, but he takes direction well. He also likes to interrupt my work with kisses, which I don't exactly mind…until we burn the first round of toast.

We laugh together as we work, continuing to steal kisses and make conversation, and then we sit and eat together.

"Why's Jonah at your parents' house this weekend?" he asks.

"We planned it months ago when I found out about the charity ball. I figured I'd either be covering or attending it, and he likes to do a double sleepover every few months. I just miss him, but I might head over sometime tomorrow to say hi." I'll see my parents tomorrow night at the ball, something I haven't discussed with Lincoln yet. I don't really want to bring it up, to be honest, but the invitations went out to several local former players, and my parents were all too excited to attend—especially given the fact that many of the Aces players are regulars at their restaurant and my dad has sort of built a name in the Aces community, likely much to the chagrin of our darling new coach.

I have a babysitter I call upon occasion, the teenaged kid of one of my parents' neighbors, and she'll be watching Jonah tomorrow night when we're all at the ball.

"You're close with them," he surmises, and I nod.

"And you're close with yours?"

He shrugs a little. "I guess. I haven't seen them much since they moved to town."

"You've been a little busy, you know, coaching. And slipping in time with your secret lover."

"Not enough time," he mutters as he pulls me against him with his hands on my ass, and I can't disagree with that.

I think about asking what his family would think about him being with me, but I imagine it's about the same sorts of things my own parents would think about me being with him. Only…my dad owns a successful bar here in Vegas now. He didn't lose all his money because of the bar back in New York the way Lincoln's father did, and Lincoln's father wasn't forced to stop playing due to an injury incurred at the hands of his best friend the way my father did. Intentional or not, that's facts.

GAME PLAY

But dwelling any longer on the topic of families than we already have feels like it'll just wedge us apart when we both already feel that wedge from so many different angles.

So instead, I focus on enjoying the time we do have. We have the rest of tonight. We have all day tomorrow until we need to head to the ball—barring an hour or so if I pop over to see Jonah.

This is rare time for us, something I feel like we sorely need if we're really here to explore a potential future together.

We clean up the dinner dishes, and then we settle on the couch. I sit a cushion away from him and perch my feet over his legs. "What do you usually watch?" I ask.

"ESPN," he admits. "You?"

"I start with the local news, check ESPN, and then pull up Netflix and let it surprise me."

He chuckles. "Really?"

I nod.

"I don't even have Netflix. I don't get invested in shows because inevitably I'll want to sit and binge and I never have the ability to do that."

"Not even in the off-season?" I ask.

He lifts a shoulder. "I guess then. But even then, I'm planning for the next season. Coaches don't get the same kind of time off players do."

"Do you like coaching?" The question comes out of the blue, and I'm not even sure why I ask it.

"Some days I love it. Some days it feels like all I was ever meant to do on this Earth. And other days…" He trails off as if to let the conflict speak for itself, but I choose not to let him off quite so easily.

"Other days?" I press.

"Other days I think an early retirement doesn't sound so bad."

I chuckle, though I'm well aware of the stress that comes with the position he's in.

"What about you?" he asks, tossing the attention off himself and squarely back at me.

"What about me?"

"Do you like what you do?" He starts massaging my feet, and I swear I didn't set them on his legs so he would do that, but I'm certainly not going to stop him.

"I love what I do. I was raised around the game just like you were, and I always wanted to be a part of it."

"Did you ever want to play? Like even back in high school?"

I moan a little as he hits a pressure point on the bottom of my foot. "Nope. Never had the desire. My preference was watching you in your tight white pants. And I always enjoyed taking part in team activities, which I'm excited to do this year as I travel with the—ohhhh."

He hits another pressure point, completely derailing my train of thought, and I lay my head back against the arm of the couch and close my eyes.

He drops my foot and crawls up the couch until he's hovering over me. I open my eyes when I feel his heat, and he's staring down at me.

"God, Jo. You're so beautiful. I can't believe this is real." He drops a kiss to my forehead. "I keep thinking I'm going to wake up from this dream." He kisses each cheek. "I always kept the hope in my heart but never really believed it would come true." Finally his lips land on mine as my chest warms with his words.

GAME PLAY

I wrap my arms around his neck as he deepens the kiss, and his fingertips start to travel along my thigh, inching achingly slowly along as the need for him builds inside me. I tighten my grip around his neck as my body arches into him automatically, as if I can't control what it's doing. And I can't. I can't control anything where this man is concerned.

Least of all my feelings for him.

His lips travel from mine down to my neck and then my collarbone. He lifts only when he gets to my shirt, which is clearly in the way here, and he reaches down to pull it off me. He's quick as he rips his own shirt over his head, too, giving me the show I deserve as I stare at those gorgeous muscles of his.

I let out a breathless sigh without even realizing it, and he smirks at me for a second before he gets back to work.

He yanks at the button on my jeans and pulls them off me, discarding them on the floor, and he traces up the inside of my thigh. He hooks a finger around my panties, and I cry out as he slides a finger into me, my back arching up off the couch as I lie here in just my bra and panties.

He yanks my panties off, causing my entire body to throb with lust before he lowers his mouth to my stomach. He trails kisses down, down, down, and once he reaches my hip, he changes direction as he moves in toward my center. But instead of moving down to my pussy like I want him to, he changes direction and moves back up toward my chest.

He yanks down the cup of my bra, exposing my breast to him, and he groans as he sucks my nipple into his mouth. I wrap my legs around him and thrust my hips at him, desperate for some friction to ease the ache between my legs.

He shoves his hips against mine. He's ready for me, evident from the hard dick begging to burst free of those jeans. The fabric of his jeans is just rough enough that I'm starting to feel the tiniest flicker of relief, something he must sense—because he lets go of my breast and starts to move back down my body.

And this time, he gives me exactly what I want.

He parts my legs and runs a finger along my thigh again, and I'm waiting for a finger to slip in but instead it's his mouth first.

He runs his tongue along each side of my pussy before spreading me open and licking my clit. He sucks it into his mouth, and I whimper from where I am, parting my legs even more as I shove my pussy toward his hot mouth.

He reaches up with one hand and grabs my breast, massaging it before he pinches a nipple between his fingers, and I cry out at the pleasure that bolts through me. He keeps nibbling at my clit, but then he moves his tongue down to dip it inside me.

I think I may black out for a second at the sensation. I'm not sure what I say or what I do, but loud moans fill the room as he hammers me with the sort of pleasure I've only experienced with him.

He moves his mouth back up to my clit, and he sucks and swirls his tongue around as the climax builds inside me. He pushes a finger into me while he pinches my nipple and sucks my clit, and it's too much pleasure for my body to take all at once.

I buckle under the heavy weight of it all, my body bursting forward into an intense, brutal orgasm. My hips buck against his face while my knees clamp together on his ears, but he rides the wave with me, keeping up the intensity on my clit and my nipple as he keeps driving those magical fingers into me.

GAME PLAY

It feels like it goes on for hours, and when it finally starts to wane, my body collapses back onto the couch, my knees falling open and my eyes falling closed as I let out a soft sigh of both relief and pleasure.

"Jesus Christ, Jo. That was the hottest thing I've ever seen in my life."

I can't force out a chuckle when I'm this relaxed. I can't even respond.

I think I might fall asleep for a minute, but I jolt awake when I feel him get up from between my legs. "Where are you going?" I whine.

"I'm getting you a blanket," he whispers. "Close your eyes and rest."

"Mm," I murmur. "Not until you've come inside me."

He looks surprised for a beat, like he didn't think my body would be able to take it this quickly after that violent orgasm I just had, or maybe it's because I just said something sort of out of character for me, but he reaches down to pull off his jeans and boxers in one fell swoop. "You sure?"

"Mm-hm."

He climbs back over me, clearly not expecting me to move, and his hard cock bobbles between us for a few beats. I'm instantly awake and ready for more, but before he enters me, he lifts me up and pulls my bra off, tossing it on top of the pile of clothes we've started down on the floor.

He moves between my legs again, and I feel his dick as he swipes it through me. He pumps it against my clit a few times, and just the thought of him jerking himself off does strange things to me. There's something so hot about knowing he's thinking of me while he does it—like that time in the shower when I accidentally caught him.

The mere thought of it gets me all hot and bothered again, and I shift my hips up so he slides right into me.

We both moan as he pushes into me, the feeling one of pure and utter bliss as we start to move together. My pussy is still wet and so, so ready for him, and he groans and growls as he moves slowly and gently over me. He's not picking up the pace, instead opting to take his time—because for once, we actually *have* time.

"Jesus, you feel good," he murmurs as he drops his lips to my neck. He lets out a soft moan of pleasure as he continues those gentle strokes, and it actually *feels* like he's making love to me. This isn't some quick fuck. This is forever.

I wrap my legs around his waist and I hold onto his broad shoulders as we move slowly together. There's an intensity between us that makes my heart feel full, like we *will* find a way to make this work together. We have to. I can't imagine a life where I never get to feel this way again.

It's just us here in this space, moving together, souls tangling together like they always have. He buries his face in my neck as he keeps moving, one hand coming up to cup my breast, and I want him to pick up the pace and drive me hard into my next climax, but at the same time, I want to savor this feeling of luxury for the rest of my life.

But like all good things, this too must come to an end. He groans into my neck, and then he rocks into me a little harder a few times before he stills inside me. I feel his cock throb as he starts to come, his one hand gripping my breast tightly as he fights through his own forceful release, and just knowing it was our bodies moving together that made him fall apart pushes me into another orgasm. I arch into him, and he pinches onto my nipple as I fight my way through a

GAME PLAY

second climax, my body tightening everywhere as my legs grip onto him and my nails dig into his skin.

As my release starts to slow, he slips out of me. He grabs his shirt off the floor and uses it to wipe me clean before tossing it back on the pile of clothes. I lay back, my eyes closed and my body completely spent now, and I feel him move in beside me.

He pulls a blanket over the two of us and tosses an arm across my stomach, and we fall asleep naked together right there on the couch as I dream about a time when what we have could really, actually work in the real world.

CHAPTER 6

lincoln

When I wake, it takes me half a beat to figure out where the hell I am.

Oh, right.

My couch.

With Jolene.

After the kind of sex that makes you so boneless and exhausted that you fall asleep immediately after.

I have no idea how long we've been lying here.

I get up and check the clock, and it's a little after two in the morning. Jolene's duffel bag still sits by the stairs waiting to go up, and it's only now I realize I haven't even taken her through the whole house. She's been here twice, and she's seen the entry, the kitchen, and the family room…and that's it.

It's a little strange, probably, so I make a mental note to show her around.

It's late, and I'm tired, but my mind is awake as I pace around and pick up our clothes. I throw my shirt in the laundry room with my jeans but pull my boxer briefs back on as I try to come to terms with all this.

I wander over toward the kitchen and lean against the counter, staring at the place where we made dinner earlier together while I try to think this through.

We said we'd explore what this is and figure out how to proceed.

I don't need to explore anymore.

I know what this is.

She's the only person I've ever had it with, and maybe she's the only person I ever *will* have it with.

So now we need to move onto what comes next: the reality.

Can we make this work? Can either of us admit to our families what's been going on?

I know exactly how my dad will take it.

And I also know I'm still harboring a rather large secret, and if she ever found out, it could mean the end of us—particularly if she ever found out that I knew and didn't tell her.

I can almost see my dad telling her that I knew just to tear us apart for a second time.

I know what he's capable of, and maybe I've sought his approval of me my whole life…but I've also spent much of my life fearing him. And I'm no psychologist, but maybe that's a big part of the reason why I never really wanted kids.

And yet…

When I was sitting on Sam's couch laughing with Jonah at that ridiculous *Minions* movie, I couldn't help but feel an odd sense of joy I'm not sure I've ever felt before. We shared something that day, and he looked at me with something in his eyes I wanted to see again. I liked having him look up to me, and I wanted to say something to make him laugh again or do something to see that look on his face again like he was talking to his hero.

But this is Jolene's kid. He has a father, and it ain't me.

It's not like the two of us can just start a life together and ride off into the sunset with Jonah on the horse beside us. We've got a rather heavy family feud to consider on top of it, and I know my mom wants grandkids, but I also know she'd never willingly accept a Bailey into her home even if he or she was half-Nash.

Never mind accepting a kid that's fifty percent Bailey and zero percent Nash.

I hate that the thought of bringing that kid to the goat farm in New York crossed my mind. How could I ever *really* bring him there?

My parents wouldn't accept him from the start, but I wonder what my brothers would think. Spencer might be the closest to being able to accept it given that he seems to have found someone himself. Asher is the closest to me geographically, but I have no idea how he'd take it. And Grayson already knows my feelings are still there after our weekend in New York. He hasn't breathed a word to anybody, but he also hasn't exactly followed up to see if I've taken action on anything yet. Still, when I told him, he didn't exactly seem surprised.

Sometimes I think using our families and their history is a convenient excuse to avoid being together. But then I think of the reality of it, too. My father feels as though he lost everything at the hands of her father. How would I feel in that situation? It's easy to say I'd get over it, but in reality, I'm not sure I would. He's a stubborn grudge-holder, and he did his best to pass that trait down to his four sons.

And what about Bailey? He doesn't know my dad intended to take him out that day in order to protect my future. But how would Joseph feel if he became privy to that information? How would he feel knowing the person at the center of why he had to endure years of physical therapy and never got to play professionally again is currently banging his daughter?

I can't imagine he'd be too keen on it.

Maybe when I retire from coaching or maybe when she isn't team correspondent down the road, we can revisit this whole thing. But for now, I have literally no idea how to make any of it work outside of our bubble.

"I was wondering where you went."

I jump at the sound of her voice, and when I turn around, I find my beautiful Jolene standing there. She's wearing just the blanket wrapped around her, and she looks sweet and sleepy as she stands in front of me.

"You scared me," I say softly, and I don't just mean now when her voice startled me.

I think I mean a whole hell of a lot more than that.

"Sorry," she murmurs, and she walks around the counter until she's standing in front of me.

I pull her into me and wrap my arms tightly around her, clinging to her as I try to banish away the negativity.

She rests her head on my chest as she wraps her arms around my waist. "What are you doing?"

"Thinking."

"That sounds dangerous." She offers a little giggle at that, but when she pulls back to look at me, her smile fades even though her arms are still around me. "What's wrong?"

GAME PLAY

I shrug. "Everything is so perfect when it's just you and me," I murmur. "And then I let the outside world back in, and everything turns to shit."

She presses her lips together. "What got to you?"

"Nothing. Everything. What are we doing?"

She tightens her grip around my waist. "Figuring things out."

"But for how long, Jo? There's so much in our way, so much at stake. The respect of my team and my staff and the media, your position and your fight for more women in this field, our families…" I hang my head a little. "How do we do this?"

She listens intently as I ramble. "We keep finding these secret moments until we figure it out."

"We keep saying that, but I want to take *you* to the charity ball instead of Sam. At some point, I'm going to want to let the paparazzi see us. I'm going to want to be proud of who I'm with. I'm going to want the world to know how I feel about you. And I don't get to."

She looks a little caught off guard, but then she poses a question that catches *me* off guard. "What would you tell the paparazzi if you could?"

I draw in a sharp breath at her question.

"How *do* you feel about me?" she presses.

Her eyes search mine, and I spot the gold flecks I fell in love with the day I met her.

I was fourteen. She was twelve. Her dad had been traded from Miami to New York, and they moved into the house next door. I was one of the only kids around who knew what it was like to have a father in the league, and we were around the same age. An immediate friendship ignited between us, some sublime and intense connection neither of us really understood.

It took me two years to work up the courage to kiss her. Another year to work up the courage to have sex with her.

And then my father ripped it all away when he made a confession to me that caused me to break her heart as much as it broke my own.

Those feelings never died. They never dimmed. They never went anywhere except buried deep down, and the moment I saw her in the present time, they resurfaced. No amount of pushing them away could ever really get rid of something this strong.

Those gold flecks are centered on my eyes, and maybe I should feel nervous as she searches to find the answer there, but I don't.

The answer is as natural as breathing.

"I love you."

The hazel eyes and the gold flecks look surprised as her brows arch, and I lean down and rest my forehead to hers. "I've been in love with you since I was fourteen, and I feel like I've been forced to spend my entire life fighting it. I'm so goddamn tired of fighting, Jolene."

"Then let's stop fighting," she murmurs.

I pull back, not sure exactly what she means by that. Stop fighting as in—take this public? Or stop fighting as in—we end it here?

"I love you, too. And I'm a big believer that *love is enough*, Lincoln Nash." She moves one of her arms so she can rest her palm over my heart, and it's beating like crazy after the words she just said to me. My chest is warm, and the feeling radiates out through my entire body like I'm fucking

GAME PLAY

seventeen again. "We will figure this out. We just need some time."

    I close my eyes as I draw in a deep breath, breathing in her orange blossoms, and then I drop my lips to her as I hope with everything inside me that we have enough time to prove her words true.

CHAPTER 7
lincoln

We spend the morning together mostly naked. She leaves just before lunch to see her son, and then she has a whole host of appointments to get ready for tonight's event—something I don't have to worry about since I just need to slide into my tux and pick up my date.

My date.

Sam's great and all, but it's really sort of a sorry substitute when I want the real thing.

Still, I appreciate what Sam is doing for us more than I can express. Someday, she'll meet some dude and want to start a life with him, though, and where will that leave us?

Maybe it'll be a distraction to the team, and the media will focus more on my personal life with her than on my coaching skillset…or maybe it'll all blow over because the next big scandal happens elsewhere in the league.

I don't know what the right answer is, but I do know that letting her go without me was hard this morning, and it keeps getting harder and harder each time I have to do it.

I didn't tell her my parents were invited to tonight's event. As soon as Jack heard that they'd moved to town, he added them to the guest list as my guests of honor.

But the truth is, I don't really want them there. I've worked hard to build my own name despite the scores of football fans who believe I got every single break I did because my last name is Nash.

Last names might open doors, but it's hard work along with a proven track record that reaps the real rewards.

Asher will be there, too, so I'm hopeful that he'll be there to run interference. I certainly have no interest in entertaining them. I'll have enough of my own shit to take care of tonight—like finding a quiet spot to bang my girlfriend.

My *girlfriend*. Shit, did I really just use that word in my brain?

Is that what she is?

I blow out a breath. I told her I love her. She said it back.

I think that's what she is, and the thought of how unconventional and backward all this is strikes me hard.

I put in a couple hours of work as I study film from last week's minicamp, and then I slip into my tux and head over to Sam's place, where a car is waiting to take the two of us to the ball.

Sam answers the door, and she looks gorgeous in a black evening gown. But I hardly notice because standing behind her eating a sandwich in the kitchen is Jolene Bailey.

She may be working the event, but good God damn, she put in the work to show how fucking gorgeous she is tonight.

I blow out a whistle as I try to keep it in my pants.

Jesus.

GAME PLAY

My dick is begging for her, especially after the events of the last twenty-four hours.

"You both are stunning," I say, my eyes drawn to the lady eating the sandwich rather than my actual date.

She sets down the bread as her jaw slackens a little. "Jeez, Nash. Exactly how many numbers are you trying to snag tonight?"

I chuckle as I rub my palms together. "None. But I'm hopeful my date will run interference so I can find a secret place to see what the inside of that dress looks like."

Jolene's eyes widen at the thought, and she tilts her head to indicate yep, that's definitely happening tonight.

"Can't you just go bang it out now so I don't have to run interference?" Sam begs.

"Sorry, Samantha, but I need to get over there a bit early since I'm one of the honorary chairs," I say.

She rolls her eyes, but I hardly notice as I step away from her and toward the woman I admitted my real feelings to today.

"You doing okay?" I ask, my voice low.

She nods, and I press a quick kiss to the corner of her mouth.

"Mm, peanut butter," I murmur.

She raises a brow. "You can slather it on me later if you want."

"Oh barf," Sam mutters from the entry.

I ignore her. "You look beautiful. No snagging numbers yourself. Remember who you're secretly coming home to."

"Only if you really find us a secret place to get up this skirt," she says, poking me in the chest.

I loop an arm around her waist and haul her to me. "Now that's a promise I'm glad to make." I drop my mouth to hers, and I give her the kind of kiss I hope she won't forget as she heads into tonight's event.

I know I won't forget it.

As soon as we arrive, I start looking for places. I'm distracted as I walk the red carpet with my date, my eyes moving all around. There has to be *somewhere*, but I also know eyes will be on me tonight.

This might be harder than I thought.

We enter the ballroom, and Jack and Steve are both there with their wives, who I've had the pleasure of meeting before.

"This is Samantha," I say, introducing my date, who has met these men at the Gridiron before but not their wives.

I glance around the room, and it's immediately clear to me how much work went into this event.

It's impressive, but I already feel like my heart's not in it. How can it be when I'm not here with Jolene?

I make the rounds with all the important people chairing this event including Luke Dalton and Ben Olson, who are here with their wives and looking like they're ready for a good time with their kids at home, and the entire time, I'm glancing around distractedly as I look to see if there are any private places we can escape to.

I don't see any. Sam and I walk outside in the gardens, and there are some private spaces out here, but none that I don't think we'd get caught in.

When we walk back in, I see a few offices with no lights on. I try the doors, and they're all locked except the very last one—the one closest to the ballroom.

Bingo.

GAME PLAY

We'll each separately excuse ourselves, make our way into the office, have a moment together, and return like nothing ever happened.

Maybe it's dumb.

But maybe I need to do it anyway.

Is it the secret that makes this so exciting? The thrill of doing something so illicitly wrong?

I mean, sure—for tonight, that's why I can't see the night ending any other way.

But when I think about holding her as we fell asleep last night on my couch, I know it's so much bigger than an illicit secret. It's the two of us, raw and pure, just like we always were together.

I'm addicted to it, and I don't know that I'll ever be able to just give it up.

The press arrives early to grab footage and photos of the event and to interview some of the chair people before the event officially gets underway, and I can physically feel it when she walks in.

Something shifts in the room, a clear reminder that whatever this is between us…it's powerful.

Real fucking powerful.

I turn around and see her as she stands tentatively in the doorway with Dave, the guy who has been with her before to film video. He's in a tuxedo, too, and I can't help but wonder if he knows about us. I doubt it. She would've told me, I think, the way she told me just after she admitted it to her boss.

I hold it together while she interviews me—at least I think I do. I've grown pretty damn good at putting on the act over the years.

I talk to a few other reporters. Other guests start showing up including players and former players, the coaching staff, the front office staff, stakeholders and their families, local celebrities including Troy Bodine of the Vegas Heat—who I still haven't met for dinner—Cooper Noah and Danny Brewer, his third and first baseman, Mark Ashton and Ethan Fuller, lead singer and lead guitarist of the band Vail, and, of course, the fans who ponied up the dough for this event.

It's a five-star event in every way, and meanwhile I'm over here like a horny fucking teenager who feels ready to blow his load in his pants if he can't get up into his girlfriend right quick.

I need to do this before my parents get here—before even more eyes are on me.

I glance over and see her talking to Austin Fucking Graham again. He's flirting, and she's smiling, and I want to fucking murder him.

It's wrong. He's a player. She's not interested.

I wish I could walk over there and claim her as mine.

I need her.

Now.

I'm not sure what comes over me in that moment—maybe it's jealousy that she's talking to Graham, maybe it's pure, unadulterated lust, maybe it's the fact that my parents haven't shown up yet, or maybe it's because people are still mingling ahead of dinner—but now is the time, and I send her a covert text.

Me: *There's an office down the hallway toward the gardens. First door on the right coming out of the ballroom. Now.*

I excuse myself to Sam, who just watched me type out that text, and she rolls her eyes.

GAME PLAY

"I'll hold down the fort, Coach," she says, and maybe I need to slip her some extra cash for being so amenable to this whole deal.

She really loves Jolene, and for that, I'm eternally grateful. Because *I* really love Jolene, too.

CHAPTER 8
Jolene

I put a fancy watch band on so I could check my texts on there if they happened to come through, and I see the one that just came in is from the coach.

I click it off quickly so nobody else sees what it says even though I've changed his contact name in my phone just in case, and I excuse myself from my conversation with Austin where he's telling me about all the potential my son has to play football once his broken arm heals, and I slip my phone out of my clutch to read the whole text.

And the second I do…

Whew.

Hot damn.

My knees nearly give out as I think about this powerful man in a tuxedo who is demanding I meet him somewhere privately right now.

The whole idea of it is ridiculously hot.

Every woman in this room wants him. The men in this room want to be him.

But he wants me.

There's something special about that, something I can't quite put into words, but something that makes me feel like together, we can overcome anything.

Maybe we both just need to get up the nerve and tell our parents what's been going on.

It's not safe to sneak around like this, but part of me *likes* that. I've always played it safe. This is exciting and out of character for me, and I kind of love it.

So much that by the time I glance down the empty hallway before trying the knob on the door Lincoln said in his text, my panties are *soaked*.

He yanks me in and slams the door behind me, locking it for good measure before he has me pinned up against it, his lips hot on mine.

Last night he was slow and intentional as he made love to me. This is something else.

This is animal and fierce, hot and carnal.

I let out a loud moan as the sound of the music pumping from the ballroom beside us drowns out the noise.

I have no idea whose office I'm in, but on Monday morning when they walk in, it's going to smell like hot sex in here. He bucks his hips toward me as he growls, his mouth all over mine and his hands grappling with the bottom of my dress like he can't quite get there fast enough.

And he can't. I need him inside me as much as he needs to be there, so I bat his hands away and yank my dress up as I pull my panties off and toss them aside. He grabs his cock out of his trousers and tugs on it a few times before he shoves me up against the wall, pinning me there with his hips.

He shoves two fingers right into me. "So fucking wet," he murmurs, and he pulls his fingers out and grips his cock

GAME PLAY

again. He slides into me as I wrap my legs around his waist. I brace myself on his shoulders as he starts to rock into me, and holy fuck is he hitting every single spot he needs to hit.

"I want to suck your tits," he mutters, and he spins us and sets me on the edge of the desk, never pulling out of me as I reach into my dress and yank one breast out of the built-in bra, letting it hang over the top of my dress while he continues to ravage me now on this desk.

"Oh my God," I squeal as he sucks my nipple into his mouth and continues to fuck me hard and raw.

I pull his head against my tit, burying his face into me, and he groans loudly as he sucks harder and picks up the pace, bucking against me like he can't go fast enough or deep enough even though the speed and the depth is hitting me exactly how I need it to.

It hits me with no warning at all.

I explode into a fierce orgasm as I cry out, my body pulsing with every plea as I say his name over and over. He comes right along with me, his entire body stiffening as he drops my tit from his mouth to curse my name. He slams his mouth to mine, growling as he comes, and when both our bodies start to come down from the edges of bliss, he continues to kiss me, slowing the pace as his tongue brushes mine in a sexy, tender, and luxurious way.

He doesn't pull out of me quite yet, but he reaches around me and grabs something off the desk. I see a tissue, and as he slowly pulls out, he uses it to catch the remnants of what he left behind when he exploded inside me.

He cleans me up first and then himself, and he glances around for a beat, unsure what to do with the tissues. He balls up a few more tissues around it before dropping them into the trash can. It's the best we can do after getting down and dirty in someone else's office.

He puts his dick away as I pull my panties back on, and then I grab my lipstick out of my clutch to fix it.

"You're perfect," he says softly, and he presses a kiss to my cheek. "Thank you for meeting me in here. I saw you talking to Austin, and I just—"

"Got lost in a jealous rage?" I finish, and he chuckles.

"No. I mean, maybe a little. But we both knew this was inevitable tonight, and I figured we should make it happen before my parents got here."

My chest tightens and my heart races at the same time. "Your…your parents?"

He nods. "Yeah. When Jack heard they moved to town, he added them to the guest list."

"Oh shit."

"What? Nervous to see them again after all these years?" He cracks a smile.

I shake my head. "My parents are coming tonight, too."

His eyes grow wide. "Oh shit."

"Yeah. We better get back out there."

He nods. "You first or me?"

"I'll go."

I peek out the office and see the hallway is empty, and first I head out to the gardens and take the door in toward the other entrance where the restrooms are. I head in there, freshen up, and fix my lipstick one more time, and then I head back to the ballroom, where I see Lincoln.

He's talking to his father on one side of the room just as I see my parents enter on the other side.

Well that's one surefire way to kill the buzz of the afterglow.

CHAPTER 9
lincoln

I'm still sweating from that hot encounter in that deserted office when I return to the ballroom. I beeline for the bar and grab myself a whiskey before I hear my dad's voice in my ear.

"Where's that Bailey girl? I know she's here tonight." He's hissing at me, and I wonder if he can smell her pussy on the fingers that are currently gripping my glass of whiskey for dear fucking life.

I clear my throat as I grapple with words, still not quite planted back in reality after what just happened between Jolene and me.

"What's the matter with you, kid? You sick or something?" he demands, and my mom turns around and gives me a hug.

Okay, it's *far* too soon to be hugging my *mother* after the sex I just had.

Jesus.

I'm still working my way down from bliss, and seeing my parents here is probably the shock back to the real world I needed.

I really need to go wash my hands. I should've hit the restroom after what we just did, and as I glance around, I assume that's where she bounced off to.

"Didn't know it was my day to keep track of her," I tell my dad. "And no, I'm fine. It's just been a night already playing the game." I give him a tight smile to throw him off the scent of why I'm really out of sorts, and it seems to work.

"I hear you. Never liked these events myself, but you know her." He jabs a finger toward my mother. "She lives for the damn things, even now." He rolls his eyes, and she playfully smacks him in the chest.

"Oh Eddie, knock it off. You know you like them too. A nice dinner, a little dancing, and who knows what the night will bring after that." She holds up her drink and winks.

Christ.

Do I really need to be privy to this shit?

"I, uh, have to go make the rounds," I say, and I bolt the fuck out of there before they get the chance to hold me back any further.

I glance around and spot Sam, who's now talking to Austin Graham, and I can't help but think two things.

One, she's a much better fit for him than my girl, though admittedly she's still a bit older than him.

And two, what the fuck is it with this kid hitting on every woman in my life?

I suppose I have to play the jealous card again, even though I could not care less that he's talking to her. I'm stopped several times in my pursuit of my date, and at one point, I see Jolene as she hugs the one and only Joseph Bailey.

I haven't seen the man in person in nearly twenty years, but he looks much the same—a few pounds heavier, maybe, and a bit older, but he's still built like a house and he looks like he could kick my ass even though I've got more muscle on me. Beside him is her more petite mother, with whom Jolene shares many of her features—the blonde hair, the petite frame, the straight nose.

The Baileys and the Nashes are in the same room tonight, and the thought pulses more than a little bit of fear into my heart.

Cocktail hour is fine, but when it's time to take our seats for dinner, I glance nervously around. Jolene is at a table with other members of the media. Her parents are seated on one side of the room while mine are on the other. My date and I are at a table with Jack, Steve, Mike, Andy, and their significant others.

I've shaken hands and played nice, and it would be even better if I could just get the fuck out of here after dinner, but because I'm an honorary chair, I have to sit through all the speeches and auctions and shit, and toward the end of the night, I have to get up to say a few words myself.

I wrote a speech, but I'm not really feeling it.

I want to say something important. Something my dad can hear but also something *her* dad can hear.

I just have no idea what it is.

"Linc?" Sam's voice beside me breaks into my thoughts.

"What?"

"Kate asked how we met." She looks pointedly at me.

"Oh, sorry. I was, uh, just thinking about my speech later." It's the truth, anyway. I glance over at Jack's wife. "We met at the Gridiron one night. She was there with that reporter."

"Oh, I love that place," Kate says. "I don't get out there enough with the kids at home, but they have the *best* brisket."

I force myself to participate in the conversation here at the table, and after dinner, I head back toward the bar, where I find Troy Bodine with his wife.

"Hey, Nash," he says. "I never heard from you about that dinner."

"Right, I'm so sorry about that. You know how it is when you're assembling the team in the off-season. How does next week look? We're between camps and I might be able to fit something in."

"We play in Los Angeles Sunday and Monday, but I'll be back Tuesday. Let's make it happen," he says.

I nod as he and his wife walk away, and I grab myself another whiskey and a glass of wine for Sam.

The silent auction starts, and we're all still in our chairs where we sat for dinner. I'm not planning to bid on anything, so I didn't even bother to look at the items up for auction. I take my seat beside my date, and we all look up toward the stage.

"Our first item is the Gentleman's Gift Basket," the auctioneer begins. "A bottle of fine scotch, a selection of premium cigars, a signed jersey from Jack Dalton, and a leatherbound journal make up this extravagant set for the discerning gentleman. The opening bid is one thousand dollars."

I watch as paddles go up into the air, driving the price up to three thousand fairly quickly.

"Five thousand," a voice yells, and I look over to see Joseph Bailey with his paddle in the air.

"Six thousand," another voice yells—and this voice is a bit more familiar since it belongs to my father, seated on the opposite side of the room.

Oh fuck.

GAME PLAY

I knew this wasn't going to be pretty the second Jolene admitted her parents were going to be in attendance tonight.

"Seven," Joseph snarls.

"Ten grand," my dad roars.

Ten grand for some whiskey, cigars, and a JD5 jersey?

It's a pissing match. A cock fight. Neither one of them cares about the goddamn whiskey. They both care about showing up the other one. Joseph might want the jersey for the bar, but my father has no stake in it. He's just being an asshole.

"Twelve," Joseph returns. When my father doesn't say anything, Joseph yells out clear as a bell across the room. "Finally letting me win one after you took everything away from me? Or are you all out of cash?"

"*I* took everything from *you*?" my dad shoots back. "Don't you dare talk to me about the past, Bailey."

The room is so silent I could hear a pin drop—but no pins are dropping given that everyone in the room is completely still as we wait out this feud two decades in the making.

Everyone wants to know what's going to be said next. Everyone wants to know who's going to throw the first punch.

Neither of them is going to back down.

"Or what?" Joseph taunts.

I glance over and see my mother tugging on my dad's jacket. She's telling him not to embarrass me.

Too late.

"Okay, okay, boys," Jack finally yells from a few seats away from me.

Part of me wanted to see them have it out. The other part of me is absolutely fucking mortified over what just went down, and I'm sure Jolene feels much the same.

"I have twelve thousand," the auctioneer finally says. "Going once, going twice…sold to bidder twelve-fourteen for twelve thousand dollars." He pounds his gavel and moves on to the next item, but it's not like I can focus on anything other than what just happened.

And it doesn't get better from there.

As the auction starts to get lengthy, people get up from their seats and move toward the bar.

I spot my dad talking to Tristan Higgins and Travis Woods, two of our star wide receivers, which makes sense given that my father also played that position.

And then I see Joseph Bailey walking toward the bar.

I rush over to run interference, to do something—anything—to stop an actual fight from going down, but I'm stopped by a reporter…and it's not Jolene.

"Care to comment on what your father said to Jolene Bailey's father?" he asks.

"I have no comment," I say, and I turn away but they're already facing off.

And I can hear them from here even though there's a low hum filling the room now as the auctioneer announces the final auction item.

"You took my entire career from me," Joseph yells at my father. "The least you could do is let me have that goddamn whiskey set."

"I took your career from you?" my father yells back. "What about the bar you ran into the ground? You took my entire life savings when you fucked me over!"

GAME PLAY

I jump in between the two of them before someone starts throwing hands. "Gentlemen, may I remind you we're at a charity event. If you need to confront one another, you'll have to do it somewhere else."

"Get the fuck out of my face, you lying, manipulating piece of trash," Joseph says to me.

And that's it. That sums up the entirety of our problem in one fell swoop.

Joseph doesn't just hate what my father did.

He also hates what I did to his daughter because of it, and there is no way on God's green Earth he will ever see it any other way.

CHAPTER 10
Jolene

What do you do when you *are* the news, but the story you're supposed to be covering involves your own father along with the father of the man you're in love with?

Wow. This is messy even for a self-proclaimed hot mess.

I was sitting at the media table during the auction, and I saw as my colleagues literally stopped every single thing they were doing as their ears perked up at the story.

Finally letting me win one after you took everything away from me? Or are you all out of cash?

I was *mortified* when he said that. Throwing taunts out that way is beyond childish. I know these two hold a grudge against each other, but *jeez*. Come on. We're at a freaking charity event, and this is not the place for it. When Jack stepped in to quiet them down, I just sank lower into my seat.

My father's name will be all over the press tomorrow.

Lincoln's father's name will be all over the press tomorrow.

My name will be all over. Lincoln's will.

And none of it is for any good reason. None of it is to talk about what was an amazing charity event. Instead, Lincoln and I will be pit against each other, the children of our father's feuds.

I'm so angry with my father that I'm shaking, and it doesn't get any better when I witness their second encounter at the bar.

They can yell and scream and act like children all they want, but when my father turns to Lincoln—the man simply trying to break up this fight—and calls him a lying, manipulative piece of trash…

That's where I draw the fucking line.

Lincoln is a good man. He's not a liar. He's not manipulative. He's certainly not a piece of trash, and hearing those words out of my father's mouth are as much an insult to me as they are to Lincoln.

They hurt me. They cut me. They slice me wide open, and even as I bleed, I know I need to stop him before he says more things he can't take back.

"Dad!" I yell at him as I rush over before he tosses a punch at the coach or his father. "That's quite enough!"

I know cameras are out and poised, catching every single second of this dramatic episode in the making.

But I don't care. I will not stand here and let my father tarnish Lincoln's good name.

"This isn't the place for this madness," I say, and I hear the begging in my own voice. I can see my father vibrating with anger as he looks upon the two Nash men—or three, rather, as Asher saunters up to get in on the fight or at least to have a front row seat.

GAME PLAY

"She's right," Asher pipes in, and frankly I'm shocked he's stepping in and even more shocked he's agreeing with me. "People are watching. Take it outside or drop it."

"Who the hell are you to tell us to drop it?" my father asks, turning his snarl onto Asher.

"The kid who was only seven when shit went down between you two and doesn't really have a horse in this race." He shrugs nonchalantly.

"I'm with Asher," Jack says, appearing as if out of nowhere. "I'm sorry, but I'm going to have to ask you both to leave. Separately, of course. If you choose not to, we will have you removed. Mr. Bailey, please go pay for your auction item first. Mr. Nash, thank you for attending tonight." He nods as if that's the final word on the matter, and he heads over toward the bar.

As soon as he's out of earshot, Eddie turns to my father with a scowl. "This is far from over."

"Agreed." My father's eyes flash as they stare off at each other for a beat, and neither one is going to back down first. So I step in.

"Come on, Dad. Let's go pay for your basket so you can go."

Lincoln runs interference with his father, too, escorting him out, and the crowd I hadn't even realized was gathered around us starts to scatter as we turn to leave.

I walk my dad over to the auction table, where my mother is already paying for the basket, and then I walk with them toward the exit.

The Nashes are just getting into a car, and my father completely ignores Lincoln as he passes by us. Our eyes connect for one quick beat, and I know he can see the frantic fear in mine.

It's reflected back at me.

We knew we were taking a risk running around in secret. But tonight's events just took that to a whole new level—a level I don't know how to come back from.

A couple hours later, I'm at home in my pajamas on the couch trying to get lost in some TV show that clearly doesn't understand the assignment of holding my attention. Instead, I'm scrolling my phone.

There must not be much going on in local news because every single local media outlet is focused on what went down tonight.

I'm skimming the third article about it *even though I witnessed it in person* when the door opens and Sam walks in with a rather dejected looking Lincoln following behind her.

When he glances up and his eyes meet mine, heat prickles behind my eyes.

I figured it would be bad, but the way he's looking at me tells me it's even worse than I expected. I turn off the television and toss the remote beside me, and I stand to face him.

The tension in here is some level beyond thick, and I brace myself for the worst.

I knew it from the start. The end was inevitable.

How can we possibly be together when there's just so much bad blood between our families?

We were cursed, and we both always knew that. Still, thinking about the actual end stabs the kind of knife into my guts that tells me even though I was expecting it, I'm certainly not prepared for it.

"I'm going to bed," Sam announces. "Goodnight." She practically runs out of the room, clearly trying to give us privacy but instead making things even more awkward.

GAME PLAY

We stand and stare across the small space at each other. A couch stands between us, but it feels like we're separated by oceans.

I don't even know where to begin, so I start with the one thing that hurt *me* the most to hear. I can't imagine how it felt for *him* to hear it.

"My father's opinion of you is wrong."

He looks a little caught off guard by my words.

"I can't even repeat the words, Lincoln. It made me sick to my stomach when he said that."

He presses his lips together. "We both know how this works. Those words will be everywhere tomorrow, and people will start looking to create a self-fulfilling prophecy."

"What do we do?" I ask as the tears splash over my lids and onto my cheeks.

He looks torn, like he wants to comfort me but isn't sure whether he should. "I don't know," he finally whispers.

"I won't let them fulfill that, Lincoln. I'll do whatever it takes to show the best sides of you, to prove his words wrong."

"At what expense, though? Your relationship with your father? I can't ask you to do that when you're so close with them. When they're there for your son the way they always are. It's not just you, Jo. There's a kid involved, too, and I can't be the reason you rip your family apart."

I shake my head. "As far as he'll be concerned, it's work. It's my boss telling me what to cover. It's my job to paint you in the best light, and I know sides of you that others haven't seen."

"You can't exactly show *those* sides." He gives me a pointed glance.

I shake my head. "Not *those* sides. But what about the side when you were laughing with Jonah right here on this couch?" I nod down to the couch I just stood from.

His brows dip together. "What?"

"You're good with kids, Lincoln. So you do some volunteer work with kids and I cover it. I find a way to capture the things you tend to hide, the sides of you that you don't let others see." I hold up a hand. "The *appropriate* sides. I show what a loyal person you are by highlighting your relationship with Sam."

"That's more *her* being loyal than me," he protests.

"We paint the picture we want others to see. We create our own narrative."

"Jesus, you sound like my publicist," he mutters.

"Your publicist?" I echo. We're still separated by the couch, and he still hasn't moved, and I hate the distance spanning between us.

"Ellie Dalton. Luke's wife. She snagged me the second I moved to town, and she always tells me shit about controlling my narrative," he says. He takes a step forward and rests his palms on the back of the couch.

"I've spoken with her. She helped run that camp Austin and Cory did, and I put in a call to her and she got Jonah and Cade in."

"She's incredible. And she's been booking my charity events for me. She's probably a good person to interview about me."

"Have you considered telling her about us?" I ask.

He shakes his head. "I haven't considered telling *anybody* about us. It's too damn risky."

GAME PLAY

"Well, my boss knows. Might as well get someone from your team in on the fun, too. Maybe Ellie could even help us."

"How?"

I shrug. "She can help us control the narrative. We can figure out how to spin what happened. She can feed me ideas for what to cover since digging into the personal lives of players and the coaching staff is part of the reason I was hired for this position."

He sighs. "I'll think about it. This is all…a lot. Tonight was a lot. I came over here half expecting you to tell me it was over, that you couldn't do this, and instead we're teaming up with my publicist to find ways to hide what's going on…"

"You thought I was going to tell you it's over?" I repeat.

He shrugs. "I wasn't sure what to expect."

"Neither was I, and to be perfectly honest, I'm still not. This couch is separating us and it feels like I just need you to hug me and make me feel like everything is going to be okay."

He strides around the couch and pulls me into his arms. "I would hold you forever if I thought it would make us feel like everything's going to be okay. But I'm not sure how we'll ever know that…or how we'll ever *feel* that."

I don't, either, and that's maybe what scares me most.

CHAPTER 11

lincoln

I drop my mouth to hers.

I was silent on the ride home with Sam as I contemplated what to do. How can we be together after what went down tonight?

But the moment I stepped into the house and saw her, I knew it couldn't be the end.

God, I love her. So much.

I can't be the one to end it.

And she wants to fight for this...for *us*. Whatever that means.

If she's prepared to fight, then so the fuck am I. I'm not going to give up on us.

Clearly our fathers also want to fight, only it's *against* each other instead of *for* each other. And clearly her father hates me with a passion he's not afraid to hide.

But maybe I've been approaching this all wrong from the start. What if we're forced to work together because of our jobs, and in doing so, we prove to the world that our father's fight isn't *our* fight?

What if they can watch us growing closer through the stories she tells?

She shows how I'm not the piece of trash her father seems to think I am.

I show that she's not the manipulative woman my father sees her as.

It's an angle I hadn't thought to use. We've been so busy with our careers and filling every free second with each other that we haven't had the time to think through how we move beyond this rut.

And maybe that's the answer. Or maybe Ellie will have additional ideas that we haven't thought of.

I pull back and rest my forehead to hers. "I was so scared that was it for us, Jo."

She shakes her head a little as her forehead rolls against mine. "It couldn't be. I know I keep saying this has an inevitable end, but what if it doesn't?"

"What if it doesn't?" I echo back in a whisper, and my lips crash down to hers again.

She tightens her hold on me, and I wish we could just stay like this forever—just the two of us wrapped in each other.

But reality will always find its way in, and it does so with the annoying clang of my phone notifying me that I have a new message.

I pull back and sigh.

"You should get that," she says, wrinkling her nose.

"I have a feeling shit's going to hit the fan," I admit.

"I know. Deal with what you have to deal with, and I'll be here holding your hand in secret."

"God, I love you," I say, and I press another soft kiss to her lips.

GAME PLAY

"Right back atcha, Coach," she says, pulling back and giving my arm a little squeeze.

I slide my phone out of my pocket to read the message.

Ellie: *Damage control meeting tomorrow morning, eight o'clock, my office. Please.*

I flash the screen at Jolene, and she watches as I type out my reply.

Me: *Damage control meeting tomorrow morning, eight o'clock, my girlfriend's place. Please.*

"Girlfriend?" she says aloud.

I laugh. "Yeah, *girlfriend*. I guess."

"Sam?"

I shake my head. "She's going to meet the real thing tomorrow. Good thing the real one and the fake one share an address."

We head to bed after I shoot over the address to Ellie, and since I railed her in that office earlier tonight and we're both exhausted after the rather interesting events that took place tonight, we both fall straight to sleep.

Without setting an alarm.

And eight o'clock apparently comes quickly when you're up late after a charity event where your father nearly got into a physical altercation with his mortal enemy.

I'm awakened by the sound of pounding on the door. "Get up! You have a guest!"

It's Sam's voice, and I jolt with a start as I sit up too fast. "Shit. Jo, Ellie's here."

"Shit," she murmurs, and then she bolts upright, too as my words register.

We both hop out of bed, and I wasn't thinking ahead or planning to spend the night here, so all I have is the tux I wore to the ball. I pull on the pants as Jolene digs through her drawers to find some clothes for herself as I pick up my dress shirt from last night.

She's really digging in there, and then she pulls a shirt out from the bottom and she tosses it to me.

I catch it and know what it is before I even unfold it.

"You still have this?" I murmur.

She presses her lips together and lifts a shoulder, and it's somehow absolutely adorable.

My chest warms and my heart seems to grow a little bigger as it fills with everything I feel for this woman.

It's my old shirt bearing the name of our high school along with a Tiger, our mascot.

I left it at her house once after we'd gone swimming back when we were teenagers, and she never returned it.

I'm a little broader now than I was back then, but I slip it on. It still fits.

I catch something in her eyes as she studies me with it on, something warm like the feeling I have in my own chest.

She gets dressed quickly as I head out to meet with Ellie, who's standing in the kitchen with Sam looking confused.

"You sleep in different rooms when you spend the night?" she asks, and she looks embarrassed as soon as she says it. "Never mind. Not my business. So let's break down what happened last night." She opens a tablet and starts poking at it.

"I have something I need to tell you," I say before she gets started.

She pauses and glances up at me. "Am I going to be mad?"

"Depends."

She narrows her eyes at me. "Okay. Let's have it."

GAME PLAY

Jolene walks into the kitchen before I get a chance to say anything. "What did I miss?" she asks.

I clear my throat. "This remains between us, right?"

She nods. "Of course."

I walk over to Jolene and lace my arm around her waist. "Jolene and I are...um..."

"I'm his girlfriend," she gushes, and I laugh.

"Yeah. That," I say.

Ellie looks confused, and she glances over at Sam. "What?"

"It's a long story, but we were together years and years ago, and then our families became enemies. We recently reconnected, but there's too much at stake for us to go public with it, so Sam agreed to be my date in public to throw off suspicion."

"To throw off suspic—" Ellie cuts herself off with a heavy sigh. She doesn't even look surprised at this point, and I can't imagine what sorts of things she's had to deal with in her career representing football players. "Right. Okay. So your dads don't get along, which is one thing, and on the other side of the page, you can't publicly entangle with someone from the media because of your position and you can't publicly entangle with a coach or you'll be accused of having a biased opinion. Does that cover it?"

"Mostly," Jolene says. "There's also this whole factor about me being a woman in sports reporting and how going public with a coach will confirm suspicions people already have that I used my body to get the job."

She twists her lips as she thinks that one over. "Maybe. Maybe not." She turns to Sam. "And you? What are you getting out of this?"

"A gorgeous new wardrobe and sticking my hot new boyfriend in my ex's face by way of the tabloids while simultaneously supporting my best friend." She shrugs, though truth be told, she looks a little tired. She switched her hours to weekdays from nine to three, and she's been working five days a week instead of three to cover the switch in her hours. She needed her weekends free to be able to attend events with Lincoln, and it looks like it's starting to catch up with her. "Except Jo and I had to have a public fight not so long ago so everyone would believe us, and I didn't love that part of it."

"Right. So what's the goal here?" Ellie asks. "We eventually tell the families? We wait for the first season to blow over and hope nobody will care about the new coach's love life? Or we just keep this secret forever?"

I glance at Jolene to let her field that one, but she just shrugs at me with wide eyes.

"I guess we're not really sure about that," I finally say. "Aside from the media angle, I just don't see how our families will ever be okay with this."

"Let me ask you a question," she says, and I nod as if to tell her to go ahead. "Why are you two together?"

Jolene gives me the same sort of look telling me to field it.

"I love her. I've always loved her. My entire life, I've tried to recreate what I had with her, but I never got it back until I got *her* back," I say.

"Whoa," Ellie says. "So that's romantic AF. And you?" She glances at Jolene.

"Same." She shrugs. "He's it for me. But my dad obviously hates him and would never approve of him."

GAME PLAY

"The same way my father feels about her and her father," I add.

"Okay. Well, my suggestion is that you two team up and do some good for the community. Show you're working together for the greater good. Your families can't argue with that, but we'll see you growing closer. A project...hmm..." She trails off as she paces a little, thinking out loud. "And you two..." She glances between Jolene and Sam. "I'm recommending you patch things up publicly." Her eyes move to me. "And you...you'd be better off publicly single, to be honest. What happens when someone eventually finds you out?" She looks over at Jolene. "Or what if you two eventually go public and everyone thinks you betrayed your best friend because she was with him first?"

"Oh," Jolene says. "I didn't really think about that. We were more concerned about diverting attention right now versus what comes next."

"Well, we can't go back now, so we control this narrative however we have to with our current events as they are," Ellie says, all business.

Damn, I like working with her.

"I'll get moving on a project that'll force you two together. First a public make-up between you two, and in a couple weeks, a break-up. I think. Let me mull this over and draw up a plan. Now as for last night's damage control." She pulls open a power point that I imagine will cover all the ways we can mitigate damage to my reputation, but the first slide shows us screenshots of the headlines in the news right now.

My name is being torn through the media right now because of what Jolene's father said, and I can see the horror on Jolene's face as Ellie shows us headline after headline.

Manipulator. Liar. Piece of Trash.

The words are used over and over, and they're painting me in the worst possible light.

My stomach twists, and Jolene looks like she's going to be sick. Even Sam looks upset over what we're seeing.

But the damage has been done, and all we can do is work to fix it. We're taking the right first steps by confessing the truth to Ellie—I hope.

But still, it does beg the question yet again: Can Jolene and I survive this?

And further, will we ever be able to tell our families the truth about us?

Time will tell, but I'm starting to think it's going to be impossible.

CHAPTER 12
lincoln

Ellie leaves, and I finally call Troy Bodine's secretary and make a dinner appointment with him and his wife on Tuesday evening when he doesn't have a game. Sam is available and Jolene plans to watch the kids, so our plan is in place.

Except it's Jolene I should be taking to dinner with the baseball manager and his wife, not Sam.

It's all wrong, and meeting with Ellie made me see that more than ever. We aren't distracting anybody with a fake relationship. Instead, we're just creating more potential problems for ourselves down the line.

And I hadn't thought of it that way. I'm not sure exactly when Sam and I should have our public break-up, or when Sam and Jolene should have their public make-up, but I have faith in Ellie drafting up a plan that'll work for all of us. Until then, we're sort of stuck in the same limbo we've found ourselves in for the last few weeks.

I have some things to take care of at home, so after I bid my *girlfriend* goodbye—both the real one and the fake one—

I get on my way. And when I pull onto my street, I see my dad's car parked in my driveway.

I blow out a breath and debate turning the car around, but I know I need to face dear old Dad even though it's sort of the last thing on my list of what I want to do right now.

I pull past him and into my garage, and I draw in a fortifying breath as I exit the car.

"Where have you been?" he demands gruffly.

"Out," I answer, feeling a bit like I'm thirty-six and don't need to answer to my father anymore. I do wonder for a beat whether he's been waiting in my driveway since last night, though.

"Are you going to invite me in?" he asks.

"I have things to do today," I say, essentially declining to invite him in. "You could've called."

"I could have, but a surprise visit is always more fun. Where were you?" he asks again, and the hairs on the back of my neck prickle in defense as I get the very real sense that he knows exactly what's going on.

"I was at my girlfriend's place, not that it's any of your business."

"Your girlfriend is roommates with that Bailey girl, isn't she?"

I sigh. "Yes, she is."

He offers a sly smile that comes off as a bit venomous. "Way to go, kid. Step in on the best friend. Knock that girl down a few pegs back to where she should be. How she got the correspondent position, I'll never understand. Like we need *more* women there." He scoffs, and I feel a little sick.

"Sorry, but I refuse to agree with that rather outdated sexism, Father."

GAME PLAY

He rolls his eyes, and then he narrows them at me. "Oh, I bet you *like* having the ladies in the locker room." His tone is full of the type of suggestiveness I don't care for.

I heave out a breath. This is exactly the sort of thing Jolene hates—having that reputation that she got to where she was *because* she's a woman, not because she's smart and savvy and knows the game better than her male counterparts.

"That's neither here nor there. What are you doing here? Can't you go bug Asher?"

He chuckles. "Asher is doing just fine on his own. It's you I'm concerned about. You're letting that girl get in your head again, and I won't stand by and watch you ruin your life over her. I put a stop to it last time, and I'll do it again if I have to."

"What girl?" I ask, and my voice sounds tired even to my own ears.

"Oh, come off it, Lincoln. You jumped in between us last night to stop the fight, and you came out looking like an idiot. Her asshole father is trashing your name and you're just sitting by."

"You think I'm just sitting by?" I hiss at him. "I've already met with my publicist. She's developing a plan. I don't need to defend myself to you or anyone else."

"You don't," he says, holding up both hands. "You're right. But allow me to remind you where your focus should be."

"My focus is exactly where it needs to be."

"On the girlfriend? Because I've seen you with her, and I have my suspicions about what's really going on."

"You can take your suspicions and shove them where the—"

He holds up a hand. "Careful, Lincoln. I brought you into this world."

"And you can take me out. Yeah, yeah. I have a long list of shit to work through today, so if you'll excuse me." I nod toward my door to indicate that I'm going in and he can get the fuck out.

"I just want to see you succeed. That's all I'm trying to do."

"Give Mom a hug," I say, ignoring his words and him as I turn and head into my house, closing the garage door on my way in to really drive home the message that I'm done here.

And as I lean back against the door after closing it behind me, I can't help but feel like he came here with the intention of making the two of us closer, but he might've just driven a wedge between us that I'm not convinced we can come back from.

It's the first time in two decades I've really wondered *why* I'm so intent on staying loyal to a man who acts like he does.

It's the first time in two decades when I'm starting to wonder whether it would really be such a bad thing to choose Jolene and walk away from the Nashes.

The only problem is that the Nashes are so tied to football that I can't exactly do that. My brother plays on my team. Grayson decided to stay in the game at least one more year, but maybe he'll come coach with me next year.

What would happen to those sibling relationships now if I chose Jolene over my father?

It's a question I may always wrestle with because I'm not sure either of us will ever be able to go all in, and the thought of maybe not having this work out between us physically twists a knife in my guts.

GAME PLAY

Jolene's working on team interviews while I'm working on reviewing film, so we don't get the chance to talk much over the next couple days until I find myself on her doorstep—or rather, on *Sam's* doorstep—to pick up my dinner date on Tuesday evening.

Jolene is sitting at the kitchen table playing cards with the boys, and she glances up at me when I walk in. She wears a look on her face resembling extreme disappointment, but she masks it quickly.

How can she *not* be disappointed that she's missing out on this dinner? It's her chance to interview the manager of the Vegas Heat mid-season. She's done reports on baseball before in her role as a sports beat reporter, but she spent much more of her career focused on football. Still, sitting in on this dinner would be a dream for her, and instead she's relegated to playing cards with a couple of first graders while I take her best friend to the dinner she has every right to be attending.

Everything about all of this is completely backwards.

Ellie's texted me with updates over the last couple days to let me know she's still working out the plan and to sit tight for now. So that's what I'm doing. But I hate it. I hate everything about all of this.

Jolene basically ignores me—or at least she *pretends* to—but I can't help saying hi to her kid, who seems to have taken to me over the last few weeks much more than my pretend girlfriend's kid.

I wonder how Jonah would feel about me if it was *his* mom I was taking to dinner. Maybe he can see through us, or maybe he doesn't want me with his mom. At first he thought it was cool, but it seems like something changed.

"What are you playing?" I ask.

"Rummy," Jonah says.

"Who's winning?"

Jonah grins as he raises his hand, and I feel a sense of pride in that—a strange sense that I can't quite understand or explain.

Cade essentially ignores me, and I grin at Jonah and bid them all a good night before I head out the door with Sam.

"Your kid hates me," I say once we're outside.

She laughs. "No he doesn't. He just wishes me and his dad would get back together."

"What exactly happened between you?" I ask as we get into the car.

She sighs as she buckles her seat belt.

"If you don't want to talk about it—"

"No, it's fine." She shakes her head a little. "It was just tough when Cade was little, you know? We'd only been together a few months, didn't know each other all that well. I thought I was in love, thought we'd make it work. There wasn't any one thing that broke us up. No cheating or whatever, we just had a lack of communication that sort of brought about the end. I was more focused on the baby and Devin wanted me to be more focused on him and we just threw in the towel. It felt like less pressure when we were apart."

"I'm sorry. That sounds incredibly difficult," I say.

"It was. It *is*. Because sometimes I think I love him more now than I did back then, but he's moved on."

I'm surprised at her confession. "Are you sure he moved on?"

"He's been dating the same girl for the last year, and they just got engaged." Her tone is flat.

GAME PLAY

"Ah. So that's why you were so amenable to this deal." And potentially that's what changed with Cade.

She shakes her head as she presses her lips together. "I wish it was that simple. He proposed after he saw that I was dating you."

"Do you think he did it because he thought *you* moved on?"

She bites her lip and it's clear that she's doing it to keep from crying. "That's what Cade indicated."

"Jesus, Sam," I say, grabbing her hand. "I never intended for this thing to—"

She holds up a hand to cut me off. "It was *my* idea, if you recall. I never intended for any of this, either, but here we are."

I blow out a breath as I squeeze her hand before I let it go. She's Jolene's best friend, but she's become my friend over the last few weeks, too. "What if you were just honest with him?" I ask.

She shakes her head. "We may teach our children that honesty is the best policy, but *really*, what good would come from me being honest about this? I'd just end up being embarrassed every time I had to drop Cade off when Devin would look at me with sympathy because he chose Maddy."

"Maddy? That's his fiancée?"

She nods.

"Or maybe he feels the same way. I mean, he waited to propose until he saw you were with somebody, Sam. Don't you think that could be significant?"

"Probably not." She shrugs.

"But maybe."

She sighs. "Maybe," she finally concedes.

I can't ruin this woman's chance at happiness. I need to think of something…and fast.

CHAPTER 13

lincoln

"How did you meet Sam?" Troy asks. "There's a barbecue joint across from the offices and she was there one night when I walked in."

He chuckles. "The Gridiron?"

I nod.

"That's a great place. You know, I actually met Joanie at a private club here in Vegas," he says. He lowers his voice as he talks, and I can't help but wonder what sort of *club* it is, exactly. "I used to be an owner, but I sold my stake to Victor Bancroft."

"Why?" I ask.

He glances at his wife, who's chatting up Sam, before he turns back to me. "There was a bit of a scandal I didn't want to be associated with given my status in this town."

"What sort of club?" I ask, lowering my voice, too.

"One that requires an NDA to enter."

I clear my throat. "Exclusive because of price?"

"And activities," he concedes, confirming my suspicions. "The invitation is open to you, of course. After the initial excitement when word got out about the club thanks to someone who broke her NDA, we've been careful about membership. It's more than just what you're thinking, I'm certain. We have three floors and a variety of entertainment options."

"I appreciate that, but if I'm correctly reading the situation, it's probably for the best for me to get through my first year here with my nose clean." Imagine the scandal that would break if *that* got out. *Coach Lincoln Nash spotted at secret sex club with secret lover Jolene Bailey.*

Yeah…not a good look for my first year when I'm trying to build my reputation—or when I'm trying to hide what Jolene and I have.

I'm certainly not going to a sex club with Sam. That's for damn sure.

"I understand," he says simply. "How's the coaching gig so far?"

"Well, we haven't played any games yet, but my boys were looking good at OTAs and minicamp. We've got training camp next month and I'm ready to dig in, install plays, and get moving," I say, rubbing my hands together in anticipation as we move on to a subject I'm more comfortable with. "What about you? How's the season going?"

"It's going well, particularly given the fact that we're coming off a championship season," he says with a wide grin.

"With the success of both our teams, I think we should devise ways to work together. Community events, interviews, you name it." I take a sip of my whiskey.

GAME PLAY

"I think it's a great idea. Have your marketing team get with mine and we'll draw some things up," he offers. He glances over at his wife. "Joanie?"

She glances over at him with an expectant smile.

"Lincoln and I were just discussing how we think it would be in our best interest to come up with some events for both our fan bases. Got any ideas?" he asks.

"Off the top of my head, a joint garage sale to clear out old inventory, a celebrity golf tournament, skills clinics, food and toy drives, podcasts, player meet and greets, tailgate parties..."

"Ooh, how about a charity car wash where players have to wash cars?" Sam suggests.

Joanie laughs. "Oh my God, yes! I love that! Maybe you need to join my staff."

Sam giggles. "Oh, I've got a ton of ideas like that. An outdoor movie night, adult themed dance party, scavenger hunt, costume party."

Joanie types into her phone as Sam throws out more and more suggestions, and I think we'll have a whole bunch of joint activities for our teams coming up real soon.

The rest of the meal goes just as well, and we make plans to get together for dinner again next month. It'll be my busy season, but this is more than just building a new friendship in a city new to me. It's also a good business move to find ways that we can satisfy both our fan bases at the same time.

The night comes to an end, and we say our goodbyes in the parking lot to Troy and Joanie.

But a guy I recognize from the paparazzi has been watching us most of the evening, snapping photos upon occasion, and I spot him toward the back of the parking lot now.

This is my chance.

"Samantha, I told you a thousand times not to worry about how much I'm spending! I'll treat you to whatever I damn well please!"

I thought about picking a fight about how she still has feelings for her ex, but I'm not going to publicly push her into something she doesn't want made common knowledge.

This, though...this could work. It gives off the impression that I've been buying too many things for my *girlfriend*, which must mean she's really my girlfriend, right? But it's also showing she's uncomfortable with the way I'm spending my money. It doesn't necessarily make either of us look bad the way something like cheating might, and couples fight over money all the time, right? It was even a point of contention when she signed the contract to fake date me.

She looks *epically* confused for a beat. I incline my head just slightly toward the side to indicate we're being watched, and even though I'm not totally sure she picks up what I'm dropping, she jumps in to play along.

"It's ridiculous, Lincoln! I don't need fancy jewelry and clothes for every outing we take. I'm perfectly content with the way I've always done things."

I take the moment to glance around pointedly, and my eyes land on the dude from the paparazzi who's been watching us. He's now filming our fight.

"Please don't," I beg him. "Just leave us alone to have our argument in private." I turn back to Sam. "Come on. Let's get out of here."

"Maybe I don't want to get out of here, Lincoln. I'm tired of you spoiling me like this. Sometimes I just want my old normal life back." She folds her arms across her chest for a beat and gives me a look that stops me dead in my tracks.

GAME PLAY

I know this is a fake fight, but sometimes this woman scares the crap out of me.

"Fine. Maybe that's what you should have, then." I stalk toward the car, and she chases after me, sliding into the passenger seat. We don't exchange a word as I peel out of the parking lot, but once we're far enough away from the man stealing photos and video of us, she drops the act.

"What was that about?"

"I can't keep up the act with someone who wants to be with someone else, Sam."

"First, what? And second…you just called me Sam." She says it sweetly like it just made her melt a little.

I can't help a small laugh. "I won't be the one to keep you from going after what you really want, and I figured if we start fighting in public, our break-up won't come as such a shock, right?"

"You aren't keeping me from anything, Lincoln," she protests.

I get on the highway to head toward her place. "Yes, I am. You're still in love with your ex."

"So what? He's engaged now."

"Because he thinks it's over with you," I say gently.

She huffs and folds her arms over her chest again, this time actually a little annoyed with me rather than pretending to be.

"If a little embarrassment is the worst thing that'll happen if you take your shot and the answer is no, then so be it. But what if you take your shot and the answer is yes?" I ask.

"I could ask you the same question," she quietly shoots back.

And that gives us both something to chew on the rest of the way home.

CHAPTER 14
Jolene

The boys are having fun living together, so I say goodnight and they probably stay up way later than they should talking and doing whatever it is seven-year-old boys do together, but at least I know they aren't playing Minecraft since their tablets are out here with me.

So I figure the boys are long asleep—or at least they're long in their bedroom together—when Sam and Lincoln get back.

I push down those feelings of jealousy that rise in me every time I see her walk through the door with him even though his eyes drift right over to where I'm sitting on the couch.

"How was your night?" I ask.

They both blow out a breath without saying anything, and then they glance at each other. Both burst into laughter.

Great. Now they're sharing inside jokes.

"I planted the first seed tonight," Lincoln says.

My brows dip together in confusion. "What seed?"

"We got into a fight in front of someone from the paparazzi," he expands, and he takes a seat on the couch beside me.

"You...wait, why? I thought you were supposed to wait for further instructions from Ellie," I say as he links his fingers through mine.

"We were," he says. He glances up at Sam. "Would you like to field this one?"

Sam rolls her eyes. "Lincoln has this crazy notion that I'm still in love with Devin."

My brows dip. So not only are they sharing inside jokes, but she's letting him in on things she hasn't even told *me*?

On the one hand, I'm hurt by that. But on the other, I realize I have no right to be. I haven't exactly been a good friend over the last few weeks. We may be living together, but we hardly see each other between our own work schedules, the boys, and Lincoln. He's either taking her to some event or secretly sleeping with me.

"Well...are you?" I finally ask.

"No." Her first answer is firm and immediate until Lincoln narrows his eyes at her. She slides onto the recliner with a heavy sigh. "Fine. I don't know. Maybe? I didn't really think I was until Linc and I were talking about it tonight."

Linc and I.

She's calling him *Linc*, and they're a *Linc and I*. It should be Linc and *I*, not Linc and *her*.

"What did you two talk about?" I press. I glance at Lincoln, waiting for him to say something, and he does.

"It's not my story to tell." He nods at Sam, and I feel frustrated that they're sharing even more things I'm not privy to.

GAME PLAY

"I told him I think I love Devin more now than I did back then, but it's too late since he's engaged to Maddy now." She says it in a rush, and I can't believe this is the first I'm hearing of this.

Lincoln *does* have this incredible way of getting the truth out of people, but still...I'm surprised she and I haven't broached this topic. I knew she had feelings for him. I knew she didn't hate him the way I hate Jeremy. I knew the weekends were hardest for her when she had to drop Cade at his place and leave, but I thought it had more to do with being without her son than with not being with his dad.

"Oh, Sam," I say softly.

"He's just...he's a good dad to Cade, and I see him now and I know it's my fault things ended. He was so good to me, but you know how it is when you're a new mom. Your main priority is the baby, and it just got hard. We tried for a year and Devin felt like he didn't matter anymore and I didn't do anything to make him feel like he did. I should have, and now it's too late."

"What if it isn't?" I ask.

She shrugs.

"What if he feels the same way?"

"He's engaged to someone else. Clearly he doesn't," she protests.

"He didn't get engaged until he saw you parading around with the coach," I point out, my brows both arched.

"As the coach pointed out to me, too." She stands from the recliner. "I'm going to bed."

I feel like I made her mad by pressing. "I love you," I say quietly. "I just want you to be happy."

She gives me the saddest smile I think I've ever seen. "I know. Back at you. Goodnight, you two."

We both echo it back.

"Ellie texted me on the way home," Lincoln says after a few beats of quiet. "She asked if we could meet here tomorrow morning around eight to go over her action plan. Does that work for you?"

I nod. "Make it eight-thirty just to make sure the boys are out the door."

He sends Ellie a text. "Done." He glances down the hallway toward where the boys are asleep. "I should go home and get some rest."

He's right. I'd rather have him sleep here, but on rare occasion, Jonah gets up for some reason and comes in my room. I'm not quite ready to scar him by seeing his best friend's mom's *boyfriend* in bed with me.

"Yeah," I murmur, and I'm all twisted up in my emotions right now. I want him to stay. I want him to hold me and tell me we're going to be okay.

"You okay?" he asks. He moves a little closer to me until our legs are touching.

"Yeah. Just a little down, I guess."

"This is hard," he says quietly.

"On more than just us. There are two kids involved, and Sam…it's a lot."

He nods. "What are we doing?"

It's the same question I feel like I've asked a thousand times, and I still haven't arrived at a reasonable answer.

We're exploring things.

We're figuring it out.

Even I'm tired of repeating it in my own head.

But what happens once things are explored and we still haven't figured out the right way to approach any of it?

GAME PLAY

My hope is that Ellie will have some ideas for us tomorrow.

Because as for me…I seem to be running out of them.

CHAPTER 15

Jolene

I'm eating yogurt in the kitchen a quarter after eight when the doorbell rings, and I find Ellie at the door before Lincoln arrives. The boys just caught the bus to school, and Sam is getting dressed in her room, so it's just Ellie and me for a minute.

"Come on in," I say.

"How are you handling all this?" she asks.

I shrug. "It's hard watching the man you love take your best friend to the events he should be taking you to, but even if Sam wasn't in the picture, he wouldn't be able to take me."

"What if I could change all that for you?"

My brows dip. "What exactly have you whipped up?"

"I have an idea that I think is going to benefit you both *and* it'll give you time to spend together. But there's just one problem."

"What?" I ask, my brows dipping together.

"We need your boss on board."

"He knows about Lincoln and me," I admit. "So anything you say here today…I could bring it to him, and I trust that he'd be on our side." I think back to my last conversation with Marcus when he told me to dig deeper into what happened between our fathers.

I haven't.

I'm too scared about what I might uncover.

Fear is a silly reason not to look, though. Because what if someone else uncovers something before I do? That might be even worse, and the thought never occurred to me until now.

Digging into something that has caused so much strife seems silly, but if I could find some answers about it, maybe that could be the key to solving the feud between our families.

Sam walks into the kitchen and greets Ellie, and she seems as down today as she did when she walked out of the room last night. She's not her usual prancing, happy self, and I have a feeling the whole Devin thing is weighing on her more heavily than she let on.

I make a mental note to find some time for just Sam and me…pronto.

Lincoln knocks on the door a minute later, and we all take a seat at the kitchen table.

Ellie is practically bouncing with excitement in her chair. "Are you ready?" she begins, and we all turn to look at her.

"I saw a clip last night of you and Sam fighting outside a restaurant. It's a great first step, and we need another fight in public—maybe one where Jolene is at the same event and she runs to her best friend and they patch things up. Keep it simple. Sam, maybe you're mad he isn't making time for you because he's so focused on his career. That's always an easy out. Any questions there?" She glances around the table at each of us in turn, and we're all shaking our heads.

GAME PLAY

"Okay, great. Next on the agenda is my plan for the two of you. As I already told Jolene, we're going to want to make this look like her boss's idea, but I think this idea will benefit both of you as well as the Aces and VG-oh-three." She grins as she clears her throat. "Here's what I'm thinking: a podcast with the two of you as co-hosts. Jolene, as a local, you introduce Lincoln, who's new to town, to all your favorite Vegas places." She throws air quotes around the word *favorite*. "And obviously those *favorites* of yours will be paying for a slot on your show, and those payments will cover production costs first with the rest going to charity."

She pauses to glance around at us, and we're all silent.

"You work together to promote charity events benefitting local organizations, you get exclusives with Lincoln to boost your ratings, and you get all sorts of ideas for features. We'll grab video while you're on your outings, and of course we'll film production to get it up on YouTube. We'll be everywhere, all social media platforms, and you'll run preview clips on every broadcast to get people to your socials and to listen or watch the full episodes. Because this will theoretically be an assignment from your boss, Jolene, nobody will question why you two are always together, including your families. You'll not just be *able* to attend events together, you'll be *expected* to." She glances around at the three of us. "Thoughts? Reactions?"

The three of us remain silent as we stare at Ellie. My jaw drops open a little as I consider what she's telling us, but it's Lincoln who speaks first.

"This is brilliant, Ellie. Nobody can argue the two of us working together for charity, and if it's coming down from her boss, nobody will fight us on exclusivity or playing favorites." He turns to me. "Can you get your boss on board and have him call my agent?"

Ellie jumps in before I get the chance to respond. "I was thinking *I* could stop by to get him on board to keep her hands clean."

I nod. "This is…this is genius." I shrug. "The two of us forced out on the town and partaking in community events together? Even our families can't argue that one."

"My father will find a way, just to be clear," Lincoln says dryly.

And I'm sure my father will, too. But a spotlight on the Gridiron should quiet those complaints pretty quickly.

"What can I do?" I ask.

"For now, nothing," she says. "I've already got an appointment to meet with Marcus in a few hours, so I'll take care of that. Let's start a group chat that'll serve as our idea log, and once Marcus is on board, we'll get him in on it too. But let's work out some details first so I can go to him with a proper proposal."

She starts firing questions at us including everything from what our schedules look like on a weekly basis to where we can record to whether we'll both need studio equipment in our homes to what sorts of restaurants we like and which charities we most want to work with. Sam excuses herself to go to work, clearly not part of this project other than the break-up with him and the make-up with me. A sadness pulls at my chest since I know she's upset and we don't have the time or space right now to talk it out.

We hammer out the major details—Tuesday afternoons work best for us both to record the show, my office has a studio we can use to record and we can also set up some equipment at Lincoln's place, and Dave will likely

GAME PLAY

accompany me places to grab a little footage before he takes off. We even come up with a mission statement for our podcast: Combining passions for football and Vegas, co-hosts Lincoln Nash and Jolene Bailey will contribute to the community with insightful football discussions as they explore Vegas and raise money to benefit local charities. And our working title? Coach and Correspondent: Aces Wild Vegas Style.

Ellie has some ideas in mind for producers who can take our raw footage and create a weekly show to air on Thursdays and another person who can pull social media clips, but that's only if Marcus won't put someone at the station up to the task. He may tap me to do it, but more likely he'll choose someone else since I still have my correspondent duties.

We draft up some ideas for our first episode, and then all three of us part ways to head toward our own offices.

It's just before lunchtime when Marcus calls me into his office. "I'm meeting with Lincoln Nash's publicist in a few minutes. Since you're our team correspondent, I'd like you to sit in."

I nod. "Of course." I grab a pad of paper and a pen as if I have no idea what this is about, and I sit at the round table in the corner of Marcus's office. Ellie walks in a minute later, and she smiles at Marcus and shakes his hand as I stand to greet her. I nearly make the mistake of introducing myself before I remember that she represents lots of Aces players, and we met before Lincoln entered the picture.

"I'm having Jolene sit in with us today since she's the team correspondent. What can I do for you today?" Marcus begins after the three of us take a seat around the table.

"As you know, Coach Nash has an uphill battle coming in as the replacement for a beloved coach who led our team to a ring last season. My goal is to keep his reputation clean, and given the events of the charity ball, I'd like to let the community see more of who he is. I'm proposing the idea of a podcast hosted by Mr. Nash, and I'm looking to partner with a local news channel for a co-host who can really showcase our new coach's personality while introducing him to places around town and giving us all a peek into the personal life of a coach. Of course we'd have guest stars to interview, and all proceeds from our advertisers would benefit local charities. Depending on the parameters we set up, we can either produce the podcast ourselves or in-studio, and when this idea first hit me, I immediately thought of VG-oh-three and Ms. Bailey as a co-host. A female co-host who is as aggressive and charming as Jolene would appeal to listeners and viewers who aren't just football fans, and my hunch is that this could be an extremely lucrative and successful venture for us all."

Marcus folds his arms across his chest and nods as he narrows his eyes at her, and I already know his answer.

It's an immediate yes.

But first he needs to ask a million questions.

"Who would generate content?" he begins.

Her answer is immediate. "Mr. Nash, his co-host, myself, and my team of publicists."

"Who would produce it?"

"I have a small staff who could handle it, or you could have someone at your station do it since you have the equipment set up here already," she says.

"And is this something you'd want to do?" he asks, turning his attention toward me.

GAME PLAY

I snag my bottom lip between my teeth as if I'm considering it, and then I nod. "I think it would be a great way to benefit the community and to show goodwill toward our new coach."

He studies me for a beat as he calculates what he knows about Lincoln and me with what Ellie is proposing. He tosses out a few more questions that Ellie already has prepared the answers to before he finally nods. "I need to discuss it with Ken," he says, naming the station owner, "but pending his approval, I'll have our lawyers review your contract. I'll also figure out who can produce this for us since you're right, we have the manpower and the staff to handle it. I'll chat with our social media team to pull teasers, but between your reporting and this podcast, I think this will be the ratings boost we've been looking for."

I feel the heavy weight of what he's saying.

He's putting a lot of pressure on me to boost ratings for our station.

I know I'm up to the task, but I just hope he's not putting all his eggs into the wrong basket.

CHAPTER 16

Jolene

Ken approves the podcast immediately, and we're signing Ellie's contract a day later with plans to get the first episode up before training camp begins.

That means we have a whole hell of a lot of work to accomplish in a rather short window of time.

Lincoln wants to get a few episodes done before training camp so we have something waiting in the wings just in case, and I'm definitely not opposed to that idea, though I like the immediacy of filming weekly so we can keep up to date on current events.

It's a Friday morning after I kissed Jonah a million times since he's going to his dad's house after school—much to *both* of our dismay, but my lawyer is still working on getting Jeremy cut from the visitation plans—when my phone rings.

And speak of the devil, it's Jeremy.

I cross my fingers that he's calling to let me know he can't take Jonah this weekend. It'll simply give me more fuel to cut him out.

Instead, when I answer, I'm met with silence. "Jeremy?"

"She left. Alyssa took the girls and left."

I can't tell if he sounds drunk or sad. Maybe both.

And I have no idea what to say.

"I'm so sorry. That must be heartbreaking." My voice is flat, but I'm at work. I'm not exactly here to listen to this dude's sob story, particularly when he cheated on me with the woman who just left him a little over seven years ago—a constant reminder anytime I think of my son's age.

"Thank God Jonah is here this weekend so I won't be alone."

Poor Jonah. That's an awful lot to put on a kid. I don't say anything because I'm still not quite sure how to handle this one.

I'm waiting on a social visit to prove Jeremy doesn't deserve mandatory visitation, and now that Alyssa isn't there, I'm more convinced than ever that Jonah has no safe zone at his place.

"I'm sorry to call you at work," he says. "I just needed…someone."

Yeah. I felt that way too when I found out he cheated on me.

I'm not about to volunteer for the position this time around. He hurt me, and I've never forgiven him for it. But over time I learned that I am much, much better off without him.

"I'm sorry you're hurting," I say, my voice still flat. "But please don't put this on Jonah." The end comes out a little more pleading than I intend for it to.

"What is that supposed to mean?" he asks, his tone defensive, and I knew I made a mistake the second the words came out of my mouth.

GAME PLAY

It was better when he was sad. Now he's angry, and he's directing it at me, and then he'll direct it at Jonah. He's not violent, so I'm not worried for my son's physical safety, but his emotional well-being is a different story completely. I don't want this to be one of those times when my son comes home from his dad's house and he's sad for two days. I hate when I feel helpless to do anything until he emerges from the fog.

"It means exactly what I just said. If you need to vent, find an adult who wants to listen. Don't make your kid miserable because you are." Oops. More words I immediately regret.

He's quiet a few beats, and I wait for him to unleash the wrath on me.

To my shock, he doesn't.

"I was hoping we could maybe…I don't know. Meet for coffee. Talk. Maybe take Jonah out for dinner together one night this weekend."

Now I'm *certain* he's drunk.

Not once in seven years has he offered to do dinner together for the sake of our son.

It sends up about a billion red flags and the hairs on the back of my neck prickle.

And yet, I find myself saying, "Sure. Dinner tonight would be fine."

Why do I say that?

Because of Jonah. If it means I get to be there as a bumper between my kid and his dad, then so be it.

Besides, Lincoln is taking Sam to an event tonight so they can have another fight. It'll be perfect if I'm also out to dinner, and then the evening will end and I can sneak over to Lincoln's place and spend the night there.

That's the plan, anyway. But sometimes the best laid plans go astray.

"Jolene?" Marcus says, and I glance up. "Can I have a word?"

I nod at him then say into the phone, "I have to go. Gridiron at six?"

"Sure. Bye."

I hang up and head to Marcus's office. "What's up, boss?"

He chuckles. "Close the door." I do, and he turns serious. "I have your podcast producer."

I raise both brows. "And?"

"It's Rivera."

"Rivera?" I whine. "After what I told you?"

"That's why I chose him." He presses his lips together. "Keep your friends close and all that."

"You want me to keep my enemy closer? Why? What good would that possibly do?"

He shrugs. "It will throw him off the scent. It'll give him free access to the two of you to see for himself nothing is going on."

"But won't the chemistry between us on the podcast make him question it even more?" I press.

"Depends what angle you're taking, Jolene. You're a professional, and I assume you'll be acting like one during all events related to this podcast since it's a station event now."

So does that mean no sex on top of the studio equipment?

I make the rather wise decision not to pose that question.

"Of course, Marcus. But—"

He holds up a hand. "No buts, Bailey. Of course you'll have chemistry. We wouldn't have you two working together

GAME PLAY

if you didn't. But that'll just be part of the picture he's seeing, and you know he's our best content producer right now. He'll put together the exact right clips to make a piece that's flattering to the two of you and to whatever local establishment you're promoting."

I heave out a sigh. There's nothing I can do, but I hate the idea of having Rivera be any part of this project whatsoever.

Though I suppose he *does* have the time since he missed out on the correspondent position.

The nasty errant thought runs through my brain, and I'm not even a little sorry about it.

Later in the evening, I pull into the Gridiron to meet Jeremy and Jonah, and my baby boy comes running up to me the second he sees me. I guess Jeremy didn't tell him I was coming, but I physically see a change in my son's demeanor the second I arrive. I wish I got it on video to share with my lawyer.

More ammo against the ex.

But I didn't, and now we're here at my dad's restaurant putting in our order. We're seated at a booth, and Jonah sits next to me instead of his father—something his father clearly finds offensive by the way he rolls his eyes as we slide into the booth together.

"How was school?" I ask, putting the attention on my son.

He starts in on a story when Jeremy interrupts.

"Yeah, I don't know what school was like for Luna and Lily today since Alyssa just up and walked out with them." He shrugs, and I can't tell if he's just trying to steal attention, if he's upset, or what the hell he's doing.

I glance over at him with a dirty look that he clearly misses, and then I turn back to Jonah. "You were saying?"

He tells his story while Jeremy peruses the menu, paying no attention to our son, and then Debbie appears at our table.

"The usual for you two?" she asks Jonah and me, and I smile and nod. "And you?" she asks. She knows who Jeremy is, and since she's basically an extension of my family, she hates him.

And I love her all the more for it.

He places his order, and then he looks at me. "Tell me how to get her back."

"I'm not your therapist, and this isn't an appropriate discussion to have in front of our son," I say pointedly.

He blows out a frustrated breath. "I told you I needed someone to talk to."

"And I agreed to dinner so I could see Jonah. Phone a friend if you need someone to talk to," I suggest.

He rolls his eyes. "Fine. I'll call my good friend Ryan Rivera. See what he's up to." He hisses it as if I'm supposed to feel threatened by that.

"Okay, good. Glad you have someone." I smile tightly, but he doesn't return the smile.

Instead, he gets up and walks out of the restaurant.

I glance at Jonah, and he looks *confused*—but not entirely *upset*.

"Is...is he coming back?" he asks.

I shrug, but then my eyes move out the windows toward the parking lot where I see him get in, start the car, and drive away.

GAME PLAY

"Let's just enjoy dinner, and if he doesn't come back, you'll come home with me," I say as Debbie sets our drinks in front of us.

"I kinda hope he doesn't come back."

Me too, kiddo. Me. Too.

CHAPTER 17
lincoln

It's another event out with my *girlfriend*, and frankly I'm ready for this farce to come to an end. I'm tired of faking it with my girlfriend's best friend, of pretending to be something I'm not. Of all of it, really.

But Ellie's right—we have to handle the media a certain way, in particular the gossip sites, and so we're here tonight pretending to be a happy couple who's also going through a rough patch.

"That guy has been following us for the last twenty minutes," Sam says quietly as we head over to the bar. She angles her head toward a man a few yards away, and I glance back at him. I'm certain I've seen him before, and I think he might be another member of the paparazzi.

I've also spotted Ryan Rivera here, and my skin crawled the entire time I talked with him. Something about that guy pisses me the fuck off. I wonder if I'd feel the same way if he'd scored the correspondent position over Jolene, but he didn't, so I guess I don't have to worry about it.

Tonight's event is a fundraiser for a local food bank, and I've already chatted with the CEO about our podcast ideas and how we might be able to work together. We've eaten dinner, I've made my donation, and we can leave soon.

But first…it's time to put on the show.

"Go for it," I say.

"Are you kidding me?" she yells, and I'm taken by surprise by her sudden outburst even though I knew it was coming.

Instead of answering, I blow out a sigh.

"You know my parents' anniversary dinner is important to me! I can't keep missing things that are important to me!" she yells, and she's really going for the Academy Award here.

"I know, and I already told you that I'm sorry. I'm not sure what else you want from me."

"Just a little of your time, Lincoln. You're always working, and I'm not sure how to make *us* work when you can't sacrifice any time for me." She folds her arms over her chest. She keeps yelling at me, and I'm trying to remain steady and calm. Maybe I'm not quite the actor she is.

"That's fair. You're right. I *am* always working, and you knew that's what it would be like to be in a relationship with me. My job has to come first." I try to say it gently, but the words hit me as I say them.

It's the crux of why I'm thirty-six and single.

My job has *always* come first. I'm not sure if that's my father's influence telling me that's how it should be or if it was me burying myself in it so I didn't have to deal with the pain of losing Jolene all those years ago, but here we are.

"I don't know how much longer I can put up with it." She storms away from me, and even though it's for show

GAME PLAY

and this relationship is fake anyway, it still hits me in the gut full throttle.

A woman is walking away from me because I've dedicated my life to the game.

But...is there more to life than football?

It's a question that has come to mind before, but just as quicky as it arrived, I banished it.

It never mattered if there was because I was content with the way things were.

But maybe I'm not so content anymore. Maybe I want to wrestle around with that question a bit. Maybe I want to feel the discomfort it pulses in my stomach. I've schooled myself *not* to feel over the years, but being with Jolene again has shown me how much feeling I've been missing out on.

I don't want to miss out anymore. And yet, somehow...we have to. And maybe that's the tragic twist on this tale.

I blow out a breath as I let her go, and I hit the bar and grab myself a drink. Last minute, I grab another glass of wine for her, too.

People are watching. And even if they weren't, it's the gentlemanly thing to do. I'll patch over our hiccup here with a glass of wine serving as the bandage, and we'll pretend to make up from our pretend argument, and things will press onward.

Only...that's not exactly how things go down.

We make up for show, and I drag her into my arms. I don't kiss her, though. I never kiss her. How can I when I'm in love with her best friend? Even for the fake show, I can't bring myself to do it. I'll hold her hand. I'll toss an arm around her shoulders. I'll pretend to drag my lips near her cheek or along her neck. But my lips have never touched more than the back of her hand. I can't do it to Jolene, no matter the cost.

And it appears that cost is higher this time than in the past.

I have a text waiting from *Lorraine* letting me know Jonah is at Sam's with her and she needs to call off our night.

I let Sam know that, and rather than disrupting the balance that's inside the house, I drop her off and don't go inside.

I go home alone, which was never the plan, and when I arrive, I have a text waiting for me from Ellie.

Ellie: *Might be time to end things. Article: Vegas Insider: A Look at the New Aces Head Coach's Love Life*

I heave out a frustrated breath and don't bother clicking the article.

Me: *I refuse to read that trash.*

Ellie: *Since it's my job to read that trash, you should know there are accusations of you cheating.*

Fuck.

I click the article.

The man tapped to lead the Vegas Aces to the next Super Bowl isn't quite the family man his predecessor Mitch Thompson was.

Lincoln Nash has been in Vegas all of three months, and he's already driving the ladies of this town crazy with his charm and looks. He's been seen on the town with nurse practitioner Samantha Reynolds at several events, but just because he's been pictured with one woman around town doesn't mean he's off the market. The public arguments this new couple has already gotten into also tell us they may not last much longer.

A former flame who preferred to remain anonymous tells us, "Linc never wanted to commit because his first love is football. There's no way

GAME PLAY

he would commit to a woman in only three months when we were together on and off for a few years."

Another source claims to have photographic evidence of the coach kissing a local celebrity not so long ago. Is he cheating on the nurse? Stay close as Vegas Insider brings you the latest updates on this developing story.

Seriously? My love life is a *developing story?*

Well, it is for me, too, I guess.

And who is this supposed source? Jess? She's the only person I was *together* with on and off for a few years.

I text Ellie back.

Me: *It's harmless enough. I'd hardly call my life a developing story.*

Ellie: *My concern is the word "cheating." I don't want it associated anywhere with your name, particularly not in your debut season as a head coach.*

Me: *I'm not worried. The two are totally unrelated.*

Ellie: *Maybe you should be. If you don't have morals in your private life, it's not a stretch that people will associate that with your play calling.*

She's got a point.

Me: *Okay…so what do you suggest I do?*

Ellie: *Podcast episode one, we need to shift the focus to showing what a good guy you are. We have a press conference lined up for next Monday to start promoting the new pod, so let's do some practice sessions this weekend. Can you?*

I have a fairly full weekend as I plan for training camp, but if it's a chance to get some Jolene time, I'll jump at it.

Me: *I'll make time.*

Ellie: *I'll be in touch with Jolene and get you some options for times.*

Me: *We can practice at my place.*

LISA SUZANNE

And then, with any luck, I can have a few minutes to…practice some *other* things at my place when we're done.

CHAPTER 18

Jolene

I keep waiting for a text or a call from Jeremy—*something, anything* for him to apologize to his son for what happened, but it's useless.

He doesn't understand how much he keeps hurting our son, and as much as I want to hold him in my arms for the entire day, I can't. I have work to do, so I drop Jonah at my parents' house for the day on Saturday then head over to Lincoln's house to practice for our first podcast. Ellie's car is in the driveway when I get there, and after I ring the bell, I stand on the porch and wait.

Imagine my pure shock when the door opens and it's not Lincoln *or* Ellie standing there but Luke Dalton.

My jaw drops a little.

I've interviewed him before, but if there's anyone who might make me feel a little starstruck running into him unexpectedly, it's Luke Dalton.

I pull it together quickly. "Luke, so lovely to see you again," I gush.

I try not to gush. Really. But it's *Luke Dalton*. He's ridiculously hot, and now he's a dad, and he's just casually opening Lincoln Nash's door for me.

"Come on in. So great to see you, too," he says, sweeping the door open wider to allow me in. He follows me into the kitchen, where Ellie and Lincoln are chatting. She has a notepad in front of her, and she glances up when I walk in.

"Hey, Jo. We're just making a list of ways to start this pod out with a bang," she says.

"Are we doing any sponsors this first episode?" I ask.

Ellie nods. "I though the Gridiron would be a fantastic place to start."

"The…the Gridiron?" I repeat. "As in…we'll need to interview my parents?"

Ellie shrugs. "I told you I wanted to start this out with a bang. What better way than for Lincoln to have to interview his father's nemesis?"

I raise my brows. "Yeah, that's a bang. I mean, or we could talk about the expectations, long hours, and pressures of being a head coach."

"All in due time," Ellie says.

"I don't think it's a good idea to start there." I wince a little. "We'll want to tease it for an upcoming episode rather than hit it right out of the gate, don't you think?"

"Good point," Ellie murmurs. She crosses something off her list. "Okay, then the first week will be O'Leary's. Our goal is to produce thirty-minute shows each week. Our regular segments will include Behind the Scenes where Jolene will ask Lincoln questions about football, Guest Spot where you'll both chat with a guest about the topic of the week, either Tasty Treats or Entertaining Venues where you'll discuss a restaurant or show that's donating to our

GAME PLAY

charity, and of course a Charity Drive segment where we'll talk about whatever charity we're benefitting. I've got a press conference lined up with the Aces on Monday, and Jack is totally on board with this."

"You didn't tell him about—" I start, but I cut myself short when I glance at Luke since I don't know if he knows about Lincoln and me.

She shakes her head.

"Okay. I think we need something interactive, too, to get fans hooked in to want to come back next week to see if they're named on air," I suggest.

"Oh, I love that. Like a Q and A?" Ellie asks.

I shrug. "That works. We could ask for questions for whoever we're interviewing the following week."

"Yes!" Ellie practically shouts with excitement, and I jump a little at her enthusiasm as Lincoln chuckles.

"Okay, let's get this show on the road," he suggests.

"Just talk it out here in the kitchen," Ellie says, and we get started with the short script Ellie drew up for us to introduce the show.

"And our first guest this week is…" I trail off as I glance at Ellie with a question in my eyes.

She inclines her head toward her husband.

"Luke Dalton?" I ask, a little *too* much excitement in my voice.

Luke smiles and waves. "Always happy to do whatever my wife tells me to do." His voice is dry, which tells me he was forced into it.

I giggle, and Lincoln narrows his eyes at me. I shrug innocently.

We manage to make it through our first practice session, and Lincoln and I plan to go tomorrow night with Sam and

133

Dave to O'Leary's. It'll be the perfect place for me to patch things up with my best friend, and Dave will catch it all on video for the podcast so Rivera will see it all play out when he's cutting the film.

Ellie and Luke leave, and I have a little time before I have to pick up Jonah.

It's just Lincoln and me alone for the first time in what feels like forever.

"Congratulations on the first podcast practice. I think we're going to nail this thing," he says.

I nod. "Same to you, and I agree."

"There's just one problem," he says, and he sounds a little forlorn as he says it.

"Only one?" I huff out a chuckle.

"I haven't fucked you in far, far too long." His voice is low and deep when he says it, and heat prickles my skin.

I'm sitting on a stool at his pub-style kitchen table, and he stands and moves in between my legs. He runs his knuckles along my cheek before he bends down to drop his lips to mine.

A jolt of excitement lands squarely between my legs as our lips touch. He moves his hands to my hips, and he hoists me up so I'm straddling his waist. I grip his shoulders as I whimper at the sudden movement, and he sets me on top of his table, which is a better height for him, as he starts to thrust toward me.

He's hard. He's ready. I'm wet. I'm needy.

I shift toward him, and he moans as his tongue brushes mine. His hands inch down my body as we kiss hungrily, the ache deepening inside me as I feel ready for him. We kiss there in the kitchen as I perch on the table for a while, and I find myself lost in him again. It's just where I want to be,

GAME PLAY

and it's a place I don't get to explore as often as I'd like. But this moment between us feels like it's everything I need to bring us back to where we need to be.

Maybe we can't tell anybody we're together. Maybe we have to hide and steal moments away like this. But maybe that's what's going to make us stronger in the end.

I run my fingertips under his black shirt and up the smooth skin of his back, and he pushes toward me again. I need these clothes off. I need us naked. I need to be writhing on top of him.

He's taking it slow, like we have all the time in the world, and meanwhile I think I might combust from need.

I move my hand from his warm skin and grab his hand that's currently trailing slowly up my torso. I place it on my breast, and I take his other hand and place it between my legs. He groans as he takes the hint, and he lifts me off the table. He lifts my shirt and tosses it to the floor, and I do the same to him. Our jeans come off next, and our underwear, and suddenly we're naked in his kitchen.

He pulls me against him, his skin hot against mine, the hardness of his chest tweaking my sensitive nipples as they brush against him.

His mouth finds mine again, and his hand trails down until his fingertips brush against my pussy. He reaches down and plunges a finger into me, a hot growl rising up from his chest as he feels how wet he makes me.

"God, I've missed you," he murmurs against my mouth, and then he scoops me up into his arms again and carries me over to that enormous couch of his.

"Lay down," I demand, and he does. I climb on top of him, and I grasp his hot, hard cock in my fist. I stroke him a few times, and he closes his eyes as if he's in pure bliss. Then I line his cock up and slide my pussy down on top of him.

"Oh, God," I moan, and I grab my own nipples between my fingers as I arch my back and move slowly over him.

"Fuck, you feel so good," he rasps, and he shoves his hips up toward me as I crash down over him. We find an easy rhythm together as we start to pick up speed, and his hand moves between my legs. He reaches down and strokes my clit as I slam down on top of him, and I cry out as my body starts to break under the intense pleasure. I squeeze my breasts as lightning seems to rip through me all at once between him filling me and touching my clit, and it's all too much too fast. The world starts to fall away around me as I focus on all the senses—his bergamot attacking my nose, and the feel of his touch, the taste of his tongue from a moment ago, the sound of his growls mixed with my moans and the sound of our bodies slapping together, the sight of his face as it contorts in pleasure beneath me. He bats one of my hands away, and he massages my breast, the rough palm of his hand making me ache for his mouth there as he brushes my clit with his other hand.

I don't want this moment to end. I don't want to give into the pleasure because then it'll be over again and there's a big question mark as to when we'll get to be together again, but I have no choice. My body betrays me.

A surge of electricity moves through me, and then it all crashes down over me as shockwaves radiate through my body. I scream out his name as I start to come, my nails digging into his chest as I lean forward to brace myself. His fingers continue their onslaught of pleasure on my nipple and my clit, and the waves of ecstasy consume me

GAME PLAY

completely as my body rides the wave of a brutal and intense climax.

He goes rigid as my body trembles over his, and then his cock swells inside me as he growls out my name and my pussy clenches around him.

We fight through the bliss together, and when it starts to dissipate, neither of us is ready to move. Instead, I collapse on top of him with his cock buried inside me. I press a kiss to his neck where my lips land, and he grunts softly at the feel as we both live in the sweet moment of the afterglow.

I wish we could live here forever.

I wish we could figure out how we're ever going to move beyond this place where we find ourselves.

But until we can, I will savor every moment I'm lucky enough to have with this man.

I don't have any other choice.

CHAPTER 19

lincoln

Sam and I meet Jolene and her camera operator, Dave, at O'Leary's for dinner on Sunday evening. They arrive first, so Dave is already set up and the camera is rolling when Sam and I walk in. It's a seedy little bar, but Jolene likes it and she's the one who's supposed to be showing me around town, so here we are. I wasn't sure if we were going to include Sam on this venture, but given the fact that these two are roommates and drama sells, Ellie thought it would be a good idea to include her.

I'm still torn on that one, but I'm not running this show. Maybe I should be.

I'm not used to giving up the kind of control I'm giving, but that only tells me what Jolene and I have is worth it. We're doing this for us. We're doing this to show our families that we can, in fact, work together. And nobody will be shocked when we emerge on the other end of it as a couple.

At least...that's the hope. We'll see if that's what really goes down.

Since Dave's at the place with a camera, eyes are already on us when we saunter up to the table Jolene reserved for us.

"Oh, you brought Sam with," Jolene says as Dave hands us each a mic pack when we walk in. They're hot mics, and I see people with their phones poised in our direction, so I answer.

"Of course I did. And if you two could make up, that would really help this entire podcast."

Jolene sighs. "Fine. Sam, I'm sorry for what I said. I don't like fighting with you."

"I don't, either," Sam says. "I'm sorry, too."

"See? That was easy," I say. "Now that we're all on the same page, why don't you show us what this place has to offer?" I suggest to Jolene.

We explore the menu, and Dave takes off shortly after he films our reactions to the first few bites of food. While we waited, we discussed what we like about this place, and the conversation moved to football for a bit, too. Sam whined a bit about how I've been working so much lately and commented that it's nice to have a night out with me even if it is work related.

It's good enough footage to send to Rivera so he can start producing our first show.

I'm ready to see where it goes.

I drop Sam off without going inside again—mostly because Jolene goes from the restaurant to her parents' place to pick up her son, so there's no real reason for me to head in. I wonder if she's told them about the podcast.

I haven't told my parents about it yet, but I have a feeling I should before the first episode hits the air.

To that end, I call my father on my way home.

GAME PLAY

"Hello," he answers gruffly, as usual.

"Hey Pops. What's going on?" It's the same line I use every time.

"You called me," he says, giving the usual line back to me. "What's going on with you?"

"I wanted to let you know I'm going to be hosting a podcast. A local news channel had this idea and my publicist signed me up before I approved my co-host."

"Oh, Jesus," he mutters. "Please don't tell me—"

"Yeah. Jolene Bailey. The station thought it would be great press to get their female sports reporter on the pod with me."

"Sure, great for them. But what are you getting out of it?"

"It's a chance for me to connect with the community, according to my publicist." I say it a little flippantly, but the truth is I'm excited for the types of connections I can make through the podcast, and helping charities is just a huge added benefit.

"Might be time for new publicity, kid. In my day, we didn't worry about dumb shit like connecting with the community."

Yeah. That sounds pretty accurate for *his day*. But we're in *my day* now, and I want this.

"Times have changed, old man." I go for a light tone.

"I suppose so. Well, good luck with it. Anything else?"

"No. I just wanted you to hear it from me first," I admit.

"Okay. I've heard it. Thanks." An awkward moment of quiet passes between us, and just when I'm about to say my goodbyes, he adds, "Be careful there. I've said it a million times, Lincoln. But she's bad news. Starting up a podcast, you're opening yourself up to a lot more criticism."

141

"That's not how I see it," I protest. "I see it as a way to connect."

"Yeah, until you say something controversial or stick your foot in your mouth. Until someone paints you in a negative light. Did you think this through at all? Or did you just blindly agree to it?"

I guess maybe I didn't. But it's too late now. I've greenlighted the project, and I'm not backing out. Especially not when it could be my ticket to solidifying my public relationship with her.

"I thought it through. Thanks for the advice, but I'm all set. I just wanted you to hear it from me first. I need to go." I cut the call there. I don't need his shit. I'm old enough to handle my own actions.

Still, his words play in my mind. What if I fuck all this up?

Because now we're working together, and it's not just me. It's her career on the line, too.

And while a romance between us would certainly boost ratings, neither of us will be ready to admit to one anytime soon. We need to plant the seeds first. We need to show the world the types of things we can accomplish together.

The next time I see her is the next morning as we prepare for our press conference.

"Usually I'm on the other side of the stage," Jolene quips as Ellie preps us in a conference room ahead of the announcement of our new podcast.

"Have you mentioned the podcast to your family?" I ask.

She shakes her head. "Have you?"

"I told my dad about it last night," I admit.

Ellie's head swings over so both women are staring me down. To say I'm a bit intimidated might be the understatement of the century.

GAME PLAY

"And?" they say at the same time.

"And he thinks it's a bad idea. He thinks you're going to manipulate me or I'm going to say something stupid." I shrug.

"Well, he's probably right on at least one of those," Jolene says, and my heart stops for a second. "Not the manipulation part," she clarifies.

"And we can fix the something stupid part with damage control," Ellie says. "We'll cut anything that doesn't paint you in a good light. I promise."

"How can you promise that when Rivera's producing it?" Jolene asks.

Ellie grins. "Because the contract stated that I have editing rights before anything is published."

"God, you're the best," I say as I breathe a sigh of relief.

"Yeah, I am," she says, playfully brushing her shoulders as she stands. "I can't edit what you say in a press conference, so let's get out there and control our mouths, yes?"

"Yes ma'am," I say, and Jolene giggles as we make our way toward the press room.

Jack stands at the microphone as we wait backstage for the big introduction. "Ladies and gentlemen, I'm thrilled to be here today to tell you about the launch of an exciting new podcast blending one of our own with an established member of this community. Coach and Correspondent: Aces Wild Vegas Style will be available for streaming anywhere you listen to your podcasts along with YouTube. Combining passions for football and Vegas, the co-hosts will contribute to the community with insightful football discussions as they explore all this city has to offer while raising money to benefit local charities. And now I present to you your new co-hosts, Coach Lincoln Nash and Aces Team Correspondent Jolene Bailey."

The small group gathered claps as we take the stage, and maybe I was expecting more fanfare, but it makes sense that we're not getting it.

After all, this *does* look a bit like I'm playing favorites in the media. To be fair, I am. Jolene *is* my favorite correspondent. I look out at the reporters in the room, and I can say with confidence that I wouldn't fuck a single one of them. But the woman on my right…I'd bed her again in a heartbeat.

And maybe I'll get to after the press conference.

Or not *bed* her, per se…but I can think of plenty of places we can do it in my office.

And now my dick is hard and I have to stand on this stage and answer questions.

This might be harder than I thought.

Both the dick and co-hosting this podcast with Jolene Bailey.

CHAPTER 20

Jolene

This is the first time I've ever been this nervous in this room, and it's probably because I'm on the wrong side. I'm not usually the person in the spotlight. Instead, I'm usually interviewing the person in the spotlight.

It's a weird dynamic made weirder by the fact that Lincoln is acting…weird. His movements are jerky and he's all stiff and I think he's nervous, too. But he's always cool and calm under the pressure of a press conference, so I'm not sure why he'd be nervous.

"Thanks for being here today," Jack says to the group of reporters who've gathered. "I'll start by saying this idea was proposed by VG-oh-three sports editor Marcus Dean, and we spoke and agreed this could be an incredible opportunity both to raise money benefiting local charities and introducing our new coach to the community. We're excited for you to get to know him. I've been working closely with Lincoln over the last few months, and I can say with certainty that we hired the right man for this position. We're a short breath away from the start of the season, and you'll be able to follow along with Lincoln in his first stint in this new era for the Aces. Let's go ahead and open the floor to questions."

"Lincoln, Jolene, thrilled for you on this journey," Kyle from the Vegas Sun begins. "Can you tell us how this podcast will be different from other football podcasts already in publication?"

Lincoln nods at me to field that one.

"It has me," I say with no modesty whatsoever, and Lincoln laughs. "We're raising money for charity while simultaneously introducing Lincoln to some of the greatest restaurants and entertainment Vegas has to offer, so we're highlighting major players in the city. This could be great for the tourism industry, sort of a coach recommendation segment. We'll interview former Aces players and potentially other local athletes and celebrities, and the focus will be football and Vegas. That's how we'll set ourselves apart."

"What sorts of segments will you have?" someone else asks.

Lincoln fields that one as he goes over the ideas we just finalized yesterday.

"Who will be your first guest?"

I smile. "You'll have to listen to our first episode to find that one out."

That garners another small laugh.

We're asked about the release schedule and how we plan to engage listeners, when and where we'll record, and who will be producing the podcast.

And then comes the question I probably should have expected, but not from who I'd expect it from.

"How will your family histories play into the podcast?" Ryan Rivera asks.

GAME PLAY

I glance over at Lincoln, and he's glancing over at Ellie, who's signaling something to him.

"It won't," Lincoln grits out. "We'll be focusing on Vegas and football."

"Not on the fact that you're dating your co-host's roommate? Because I'd imagine that would give you some great drama to discuss on air," he presses.

"Vegas and football," Lincoln repeats.

"Would you like to comment on the cheating allegations recently published about you?"

I could punch Ryan when he asks that.

What the hell kind of question is that—especially coming from a colleague of mine? It makes him look bitter and petty.

I've sat in enough of these press conferences that I know how to handle it, though.

"That's unrelated to the podcast," I say, and I offer a smile. "Do we have any other questions related to the podcast?"

We field a few more, and then we say our goodbyes as we tell everyone to tune in on Wednesday for our first episode.

Ellie meets us in a conference room to recap afterward, and Lincoln is pacing while I sit perched on the edge of a table, my fingers digging into the soft wood underneath.

"You both did amazing," she says with a big smile when she walks in, and I'm not sure if it's just lip service or if she really believes it went well.

"That fucking Rivera. Why did your boss think he's the right guy to produce this?" Lincoln asks.

I shake my head. "Something about keeping my enemies close," I mutter.

"He's already trying to make us look like fools," he protests.

"I won't let him," Ellie assures us both.

I don't have a good feeling about it, though.

Ellie goes over a few things, and then she heads out. She does, after all, have other clients to take care of, and Lincoln has been eating up a lot of her time recently.

"Do you have a minute for a quick meeting in my office?" Lincoln asks.

I raise a brow. "A meeting?"

"A press conference plus you in a skirt make me horny."

I laugh. "Yeah, I think I can make time for one of *those* kinds of meetings." I follow him toward the back elevator, and once we're sealed alone into privacy, I can't help but murmur, "So press conferences do it for you, huh?"

He hits the button to make the elevator stop, and he stalks over to me in my corner of the elevator. "*You* do it for me, Bailey."

I'm surprised he called me by my last name, and he looks taken aback for a second, too. It very nearly ruins the moment between us. It's almost like if we can pretend we're not related to the mess between our families, if we can just disassociate, we'll be okay.

But that's not the case.

Still, he plows forward, putting the word behind us, and his lips crash down to mine. He only kisses me for a beat before he moves his lips down my neck and into my cleavage, and then he moves further down and pulls my panties down my legs. He deposits them into his pocket then lifts one of my legs up, tosses it over his shoulder, and proceeds to make a meal of my pussy right there on the elevator.

Mirrors are all around us, and I watch as he licks and sucks my pussy. It's like something out of some hot porn as

GAME PLAY

I watch him in the mirrored glass, my leg up over his shoulder, his face buried between my legs, my soft moans as his tongue slides in and out of me before sucking on my clit.

His breath catches when he slips his tongue inside me, and the thought that he's so overwhelmed with my body and my taste is such a turn on that I nearly slip into my climax. I fight it off, stifling a moan as I grab the back of his head and push him further into my pussy. He groans softly, the hum mixed with the scruff on his jaw pure magic against my raw, wet skin, and then the elevator jolts to a start again.

His tongue presses onto my clit when the elevator halts, and *fuck* I'm so close but I think we've arrived on his floor and the doors are about to open. He unhooks my leg from his shoulder and sets it gently to the floor as he straightens to a stand just as the doors glide open, and who else would be standing there as if they just stepped off the other elevator but Jack Dalton and Steve Shanahan?

Lincoln's chin glistens with the wetness from my pussy, and I swear they each give us a look that tells me they *totally* know what we were doing in there but I can't really acknowledge it because I'm so damn close to exploding right now.

Just one mere flick of my clit might do the trick, and I scurry off the elevator as Lincoln exchanges pleasantries with the high-powered men as if he doesn't have my panties in his pocket, and I do everything in my power to remain cool through the searing ache between my legs.

But it's nearly impossible…especially when I'm not wearing any underwear.

"Great job at the press conference," Jack says, and I'm not sure if he's addressing me or Lincoln, but I can't look up at him because every time I take another step, there's the tiniest measure of friction sending jolts of need through me.

"Thanks," Lincoln answers for both of us. "It seemed well-received given our audience."

How he maintains his cool in this moment is beyond me.

"I was talking to Jolene," Jack says with a smirk.

"Oh, I, uh…" I'm sputtering as I try to form words that aren't purely moans. "Thanks." I finally manage the single word, and I'm pretty damn proud of myself.

"Where are you two off to?" he asks.

Sex in his office.

"We have a few details to go over before we record our first episode tomorrow," Lincoln answers, thankfully fielding that one since my brain is currently malfunctioning.

"We'll let you get to it. I'll see you this afternoon," he says to Lincoln with a nod. "Always a pleasure, Ms. Bailey," he says to me, and then he and Steve head in the opposite direction as I practically run with Lincoln toward his office.

We have one remaining obstacle, and that's Megan.

"Hey, Coach," she says brightly. "You have a three o'clock with Jack and Steve, but you're clear until then. I have three emails for your review and two players who want to meet with you. Can I send them up?" She glances at me with a bit of a question in her eyes.

"Jolene and I are working out a few podcast details. Should take us, oh, maybe twenty minutes?"

I raise both brows. I'll be done in about twenty seconds if I'm being honest. I nod because I'm still having trouble forming words.

"Right. I'll give you a half hour," Megan says, and I swear she shoots me a knowing glance.

I suppose these doors aren't soundproof.

GAME PLAY

"Thanks, Megan," Lincoln says to her, and then he ushers me into his office with his hand on the small of my back.

He slams the door shut behind us and no sooner is it latched shut than his lips crash to mine.

He tastes like the tang of my pussy, and somehow the thought of what he just did to me in that elevator has me practically climbing him with need. I deepen the kiss, picking up the pace as I shove my tongue further into his mouth, and he seems to like that I'm crazy with need for him. He dishes it right back as he starts to buck his hips toward me, that thick, hard cock coming at me over and over and over. It's exactly what I need from him, and he shoves my skirt up then sets me on the edge of his desk.

He fumbles with his belt for a beat then pulls his cock out, and he slides it right into me without another word between us. I wrap my legs around his waist as I lean back, shifting my hips as he drives into me. I glance down at our connection and see where he's plowing into me over and over, and just the mere sight of it is enough to push me over the edge.

I cry out as I start to come, and I'm about to fall back onto the desk when he reaches around to hold me. He crushes me against him as I fight through the climax, and he hammers into me, not letting up or slowing down as he searches for his own release. Just as my body stops pulsing over his, he bucks harder twice before he freezes and lets out the hottest growling sound I've ever heard in my life.

He comes violently into me, and I grip onto him the same way he held me through my own orgasm. Something about holding onto each other in the most carnal time two people can share is both intimate and erotic.

We're not even naked. We've barely shed enough clothes to do this, and yet it's still one of the hottest moments of my life.

We're both panting as we come down from the bliss, and eventually he pulls out. He grabs a tissue to clean up the mess he made.

"Can I have my underwear back now?" I ask, and he chuckles.

And then he shakes his head. "They're my souvenir from our first press conference together."

"Oh my God, Lincoln. That's…"

"Hot?" he guesses.

"I was going to say gross, but you do you."

My words earn a laugh, and it's the type of sound I'll never get tired of hearing.

We don't really have any podcast stuff to discuss, but I know he has work to do. And I do, too.

So he kisses me one more time with the kind of kiss that tells me what we just did meant as much to him as it did to me, the kind of kiss I'll be able to hold onto until we see each other again, and then I duck out of his office and wave goodbye to Megan, who definitely knows there's something more than a podcast going on in that office.

Without my panties.

CHAPTER 21

lincoln

Our goal is to record the entire podcast in under an hour since I won't have time once the season starts for much more than that, and somehow the stars align this week to make it work. We send the footage to the station so Rivera can produce it into our half-hour show, and we're on pins and needles waiting to hear the approval from Ellie on Wednesday morning so we can officially publish our first episode by five o'clock.

The approval comes through a little before nine.

I'm at the office, and I assume Jolene is at hers, too.

Ellie: *It's incredible. I'm so proud of you both. The chemistry between you two is chef's kiss and I'm so excited about the incredible opportunities this is going to open for you both to partner with the community. Congratulations!*

Lorraine: *Oh, thank God. What a relief. I've been nervous since we sent the footage to Rivera yesterday.*

Me: *WTF is chef's kiss?*

Ellie: *[eyeroll emoji] Perfection.*

Well, that seems to be good news. I glance up at the doorway when I see movement only to find Asher standing there as he lifts a fist to knock on the frame.

"Come on in," I say.

He glances at me and then back at the door as he steps in. "Can I close it?"

I nod, and he does before he walks over to slide into the chair opposite me.

"What's going on?" I ask. The way he's sort of just collapsed in a chair is a little worrisome, but my brother tends to be unpredictable, so I never really know what I'm going to get out of him.

"Two things," he says.

I raise my brows.

"First, has Mom talked to you at all?"

"About what?" I ask.

He shrugs. "She texted me last night looking for Dad. I was just curious if she hit you up, too."

"Looking for Dad? Like he disappeared?" I'm confused as I try to clarify what he's asking.

"I guess he told her he was meeting me for drinks and he was out longer than she was expecting and not getting back to her. So she hit me up."

"Was he with you?" I ask.

He shakes his head. "Not sure why he would've involved me in whatever lie he's telling."

"Yeah, that seems a little suspect, but let's not jump to any conclusions. What's the second thing?"

"Wait. You don't want to, like, dissect what the fuck is going on with our parents?" he asks.

GAME PLAY

I chuckle. "Not really. If Dad's getting some ass on the side, that's between them and not something I need taking up space in my brain."

He makes a face like he's going to barf at the thought of it.

"See? That's why I don't need it taking up brain space. So what else did you need to discuss?"

"Can I borrow some cash?" he asks.

I lean back in my chair. "Borrow some cash? For what?"

"I may have made a dumb bet and gotten myself into a little trouble."

I heave out a sigh. Maybe bringing my little brother to Vegas wasn't the best move, but once camp starts in a few weeks, he won't have time to make stupid bets. "How much are we talking?"

"Two fifty."

"Two hundred fifty dollars?" Yeah, that I can swing.

"Two hundred fifty *thousand* dollars," he clarifies.

I balk at that. "What the fuck kind of bet did you make?"

"Look, I could go somewhere else and get more people involved, or you can just fork it over and we call it a day."

"You say *borrow* as if you'll pay it back," I say.

"And I will. You know I'm good for it."

I sigh. He signed a contract with guaranteed money, but the signing bonus is to be paid out in equal installments. So he's gotten *some* of his guaranteed money, but not all of it yet.

I don't want to get involved, and my gut tells me this is a dumb idea...but he's more than just some player on my team. He's my little brother, and I feel responsible for him in a way that I don't feel about my other players.

I want to take care of him...and I don't want him causing trouble in the off-season when we're weeks away from making our first impression as two brothers on the same team. It's the first time a head coach has coached his brother, and people will be watching us closely this season because of it.

"Fine," I mutter. "I'll talk to my financial manager and get it to you by the close of business today."

"Thanks, man. You're a real lifesaver." He stands to leave, and I shake my head.

I give him the look that says sit your ass back down, and he does.

I lean forward and lower my voice to a hiss. "I'll give you the money, but I need to know what kind of bet you made that costs a quarter of a million dollars. It's not just you out there, you know. You're representing me, too, and I don't need you making me look like an idiot because you can't handle yourself."

"I know, I know. I fucked up, okay? I got in over my head in a high-stakes poker game."

"Yeah, I'd say that's fucking up pretty badly."

"I started with a good run, and it just..." he shrugs. "It got out of hand fast. They were pros and they saw how they could shake me down." He's pleading innocence, but I don't buy it.

"Fine," I say, giving him the benefit of the doubt. "But don't involve anyone else, and for fuck's sake, don't do it again."

"I won't. Thanks for helping me out, man," he says as he rises to a stand. "I promise to pay you back, and I promise I won't let you down again."

GAME PLAY

"You're goddamn right about that. Now get downstairs and put in some work in the training room." I'm snarling and cranky, but his mistake just cost me a whole lot of money.

He made two promises there. He'll pay me back, and he won't let me down again.

If *I* were the betting man in this situation, I wouldn't put money on him keeping either of those promises.

Before he walks out of my office, he turns back toward me. "Oh, one more thing. Your secretary…is she single?"

I roll my eyes. "Get the fuck out of here."

He scampers out, but I definitely hear him chatting up Megan instead of heading down to the training room as I suggested.

I'm starting to regret bringing Asher in, but I know his performance on the field will speak for itself. I just need to get him safely to the start of the season. It's only a few weeks. I can do this.

But my parents? That could be an entirely different story.

CHAPTER 22

Jolene

Our podcast has been out for two days and it's the third most listened to podcast on Spotify. I think I might be in shock.

I knew it would be good, but it turned out even better than we had imagined. Reviews are rolling in, and it seems to be unanimous: the chemistry between us just rolls through the airwaves.

It's hard to deny something quite this powerful.

But that also means if everyone else is hearing it in our voices, well...my parents might be, too. And that could pose a problem for me even if it's just personal.

But it prompts me to text my mom and invite Jonah and myself over for dinner tonight, but before her response comes through, Rivera shows up at my cubicle.

It should be a celebratory visit given the hand he had in creating the final product that's being so well-received, but I just don't see myself ever getting on the same page as Rivera so that we could have that sort of celebration.

"I saw it in your eyes," he says casually.

My brows dip together as I glance up from the document I'm working through. "Saw what in my eyes?"

"You're in love with him. And I'm not sure if he feels it back, but the way everyone is talking about the chemistry between you, I have to believe he does. I'm not sure why, but that's another matter entirely."

"You're not sure why?" I ask, ignoring the rest of his speech.

"Yeah. I'm not sure why he'd want *you* of all people, but I guess he does." He shrugs. "At least the way he was eating your face that night made me think he does."

"Eating my face?" I repeat as I make a face. "That's a lovely picture, and you're sure creating quite the fictional story, but I think it's time to let it go. We're working together on a podcast. He's dating my best friend. There's nothing more to it."

"You keep saying that, and yet I have the photographic evidence that there *is* something more."

"*Was*," I say firmly.

"I know what's going on, and I will do whatever it takes to prove I'm right," he threatens.

"What good is that going to do? You're going to come out looking like an asshole either way." I say the words coolly, doing my best to appear unruffled, but the truth is…I'm ruffled.

"Not when I prove I'm right."

I blow out a breath, ready with a retort, when Marcus comes rushing up to us. "Oh, good, you're both here. I need to go. I, uh—" He's flustered, his eyes darting all around the room, and it's setting me further on edge. "I just got word that my mother had a bad fall and she broke her hip. I need to get to her."

"Of course," I say, standing to offer my support. "What can we do?"

"I'm not sure yet. I, uh…I don't have any siblings and my dad is long gone, so I'm all she has."

"I'm so sorry, Marcus," I say.

He nods, brushing off my sympathy. "It's fine. I just…I need to get home and figure things out with Sabrina and the kids."

GAME PLAY

"Where's your mom located?" I ask, and Rivera is suspiciously quiet during the entire exchange.

"Florida."

"Will you just need to be there for the surgery?" I'm trying to maintain my sympathy but I still need to know how long my boss is going to be out.

"I have to make the cross-country trip, be with her during the surgery and help her after in rehab, sell her place and get her set up in an assisted living facility. I have no idea how long that might take. A few weeks, probably. I can work semi-remotely, in fact I will *need* to, but I'll need your help here." He looks between Rivera and me. "Jolene," he begins, and I figure he's going to ask me to be in charge here in his absence, "with the podcast and the season starting soon, your plate is full. Ryan, I'll need you to step in as the temp editor while I'm out."

I gasp audibly, not really caring that Rivera overhears me. "Are you serious?"

"It's my only option. I need to go. Please tell me you two can play nice while I'm away," he says.

"I know I will," Rivera says, his lips so far up Marcus's ass he can probably taste what he had for lunch.

I cross my arms over my chest defensively. "Fine," I mutter.

I don't like any of this one tiny bit, and I don't trust Rivera at all.

I'm a little worried about what he might do in Marcus's absence, but there's nothing I can do about it, and it's not like I can unload Rivera's threats onto Marcus now that he's worried about his mom.

I keep my mouth shut and cross my fingers as I hope for the best.

After Jonah gets home from school, we head over to my parents' house. His favorite thing to do is sit in my dad's office watching all the YouTube channels I don't allow at home, and once he's set up in there, my parents sit in the kitchen with me as we each crack open a soda, my mom's preferred beverage of choice.

"Heard about the podcast," my dad says gruffly.

"Yeah, I figured you did. It's sort of why I decided to stop by for dinner."

"Do you think partnering with that monster is a good idea after what he did to you?" he presses.

"He's not a monster, Dad," I say, and my voice sounds tired. "Can't we just put the past back where it belongs?"

"I went through the worst injury of my life at the hands of Eddie Nash, the man who claimed to be my best friend. He ended my career, Jolene. Do you understand that?"

"Of course I do," I begin, but he barges on over my words.

"His son tore your heart out and stepped all over it the same goddamn day. If you think for one hot second I'm going to bury that in the past, you are mistaken. They will do it again. You just watch. This supposed *chemistry* between you two—it's for ratings. Lincoln Nash is putting on an act. I'm sorry to tell you but if you get close to him again, he will only hurt you again. That's the reality of it, and I can't stand by supporting this." He storms out of the room without waiting for a response.

I glance at my mom, who remained silent through that entire exchange, and I wait for her to say something supportive.

But that's not what I get.

She sighs and shakes her head a little as she presses her lips together. "I'm with your father, honey."

My brows crease together. "You're with him? Seriously? Don't you care about my career?"

"I care about your heart, baby girl." She pats her chest. "Seeing your child with a broken heart is one of the worst things a parent can endure, and you changed after he broke up with you. You've never been the same. I can't watch you go back down that road."

GAME PLAY

"We're hosting a podcast, Mom! It's not like we're sleeping together!"

But that's the thing.

We are.

And it's further confirmation that my parents will never be okay with it.

At some point, I'm going to have to make a choice.

Do I break up my entire family dynamic and the close relationship my son has with my parents? Or do I follow my heart?

I know what I want to do...but I'm becoming more and more convinced that what I want isn't what I'll get.

CHAPTER 23
lincoln

"Everything okay with you and Dad?" I ask my mother over the phone later that night after the wire transfer to Asher goes through.

She sighs. "Fine, honey. Why do you ask?"

"Asher said you called him looking for Dad. Just curious what's going on."

"Oh, you know your father. Turns out he told me he was meeting Asher when he really went to the casino. He didn't want me to know he was gambling again."

The *oh, you know your father* line throws me a bit. Do I know him at all? I'm surprised he went to the casino without her, even more surprised he lied about it, and some level above surprised but below shocked that she said he's gambling *again*.

"What do you mean by *again*?" I ask.

"He got into some trouble a few years ago when we were in Vegas. Some private poker game," she says, but she doesn't share more than that.

Apparently the apple doesn't fall far from the tree.

In fact, I can't help but wonder whether Asher and my dad actually *were* together last night—for part of the night, at least.

"I listened to your podcast," she says. "Just so you know. Dad didn't, though. But I love that you're giving back to the community. You're a good boy."

I chuckle. Nobody has called me a good boy in years.

"I just wish it was with anybody else," she admits. I don't bother commenting. I know her feelings on the Bailey family. She and Joanna were best friends before Joseph's injury, and between my dad, my mom, and me, we all lost someone important to us that day. My mom lost her best friend. I lost my girlfriend. And my dad didn't just lose his best friend. In many ways, he also lost his son. And further down the road, he lost his restaurant, his money, his self-respect.

All because of one stupid move.

So maybe he has a right to hate the Baileys, but if he does, he should also consider who was the central source of all that loss.

"Anyway," she says, brushing that last statement into the past, "if there's anything I can do, just let me know. I'd love to give back to the community, too, in particular since I'm new here. I haven't made any friends yet, and I'm stuck here with your father doing who knows what."

"Sure, Mom," I say, and I can't help the next question. "Are you happy you moved here?"

I think I mean to ask whether she's happy with my father, but that's not the question that comes out. Maybe I'm too afraid to hear the answer. I may be in my mid-thirties, but that doesn't mean I want to see my parents break up.

GAME PLAY

But the more I think about it…the more I wonder whether they'd be happier that way.

Because I'm not the only one who changed that day. My mom did, too, and it's hard to imagine that these two who got married so damn young are still the same people they were forty years ago.

"To be determined," she says.

We all go through changes in our lives, and I suspect my parents have grown in opposite directions over the years. They were teenagers when they met. It's hard to imagine they grew together in every way over the four decades they've been together.

But on the other hand…I can't help but wonder whether Jolene and I *did* grow together even though we were apart. I think we share a lot of the same values, but we've been so busy fucking in the time we have together that we haven't spent much time talking about what we want out of the future—and whether that future will be shared together or not.

I think it's too big a question to answer right now, but the more time I spend with her, the more I see a future that includes her.

But I can't see both her and my father in the same picture, so at some point, I'll have to make a choice.

"What will be the determining factor?" I ask.

"Seeing my boys on the field together at games."

"You need a life separate from your boys, Mom," I chide.

"I know. I'll find my place. I guess I just got used to hanging with the goats on the farm, and life's a little more fast-paced here."

"Why don't you go back to New York, then?"

She clears her throat. "Your father put the farm up for sale."

"He what?" I choke. Grayson and I paid off the farm so my mom could have it forever. Spencer pays the staff. And my father just…put up the farm without telling us?

"You heard me correctly." She's quiet a beat. "Anyway, I better go, honey. Let me know if there are any charity events for an old lady like me."

"You're hardly old, Mom."

She practically snorts at me. "Even if one of you surprised me with grandchildren at this point, I'm not sure I could keep up."

"Oh stop it," I tease, but I'm only saying it because I'm deflecting what I already know is the next question.

"So when will that happen, by the way?"

Predictable…as is my answer. "Not anytime soon."

She sighs with exaggerated disappointment, and we say our goodbyes.

Still, that call gave me an awful lot to think about, and maybe the topic at the forefront of my mind is whether my parents are destined to stay together forever or if there's an end in sight…and what that will mean for their four adult children.

Maybe nothing.

But maybe they'll force us to choose sides when I'm already caught in the middle of a situation where I'll need to choose sides.

I don't want them to separate. I don't want them to go through the hardship that certainly comes with divorce.

Still, I can't help but think that if they do, it might just make my own decisions that much easier.

CHAPTER 24

Jolene

Our second episode dropped two days ago, and it hit the number two spot for sports podcasts this week. I'm thrilled with what we've already accomplished, and training camp is just two weeks away so Ellie has filled both our calendars with charity work that we can spread out through our next few weeks.

It's great since that means I get more public time with Lincoln.

But it also sucks because we're still hiding our real feelings in public.

And I have to be extra careful since Rivera is acting as my boss in my real boss's absence.

It's Friday morning, and I suppose I should've called Jeremy before this moment, but I decided to hold out to see if he'd call first. It's his weekend with Jonah, and the last time we saw him was when he stormed out of the Gridiron two weekends ago.

He answers right away, and he sounds like he's in a much better mood than he was the last time we saw him. Still, alarm bells ring. I don't like the moodiness and the unpredictability of it all.

"Jolene, hi. What can I do for you?"

"I haven't heard from you and just wanted to chat about this weekend," I say, careful with both my words and my tone.

"Right, sure. Listen, I can't talk now but we're excited for Jonah to get here. We have fun plans this weekend."

"We?" I ask.

"Oh, right. I didn't tell you. Alyssa came back. She was mad at me, but we patched things up and we're in a better place now," he says. "I promised not to stay so late at work, and Alyssa promised to be more understanding."

I don't know what to believe. On the one hand, I want it to be true. I want my son to be able to go over and see his dad and not worry about what sort of emotional state his father will be in.

On the other hand…he's not exactly been truthful and forthcoming, so I'm a bit confused.

"That's great," I say. "What are the weekend plans?"

"Wet'n'Wild all day Saturday, and Alyssa scored some aquarium tickets for Sunday," he says, and I'm glad he actually has plans for Jonah while he's there.

"Jonah will love all that," I say.

"So will the girls. And I'm sorry about the Gridiron. I was in a bad place. I should've called to apologize before now."

"Your son is the one who deserves the apology," I say.

"I'll work on it this weekend."

I sigh. I sure hope so.

I text Lincoln to let him know Jonah is going to his dad's place this weekend, and he texts me back to let me know that means I'll be staying with him this weekend.

GAME PLAY

After his event with Sam tonight, of course.

I can't pretend I'm not thrilled for the chance at some extended alone time with him. We've barely had time to connect outside of the stuff Ellie's got us doing for the podcast, and it's hard enough having a secret affair, but add all these other pressures on top of it and I'm starting to feel the distance looming between us.

I'm just ready for the season to get underway. I'm ready for training camp, and I glance back at the email I received just a few minutes ago from Marcus.

Jolene,

Great news. You were approved to travel with the team to California for training camp. We won't send a camera crew with you but you can take whatever equipment you want with. We'll do a behind the scenes miniseries showcasing camp with a focus on the new coaching staff, rookies, and how the new team is coming together. The Aces should be in touch with your travel arrangements.

Marcus

Two weeks away with the team sounds incredible...but two weeks away from my son sounds like hell.

I'll need to figure out arrangements for Jonah while I'm gone. I know Sam will volunteer to do whatever I need her to do, but it's an awful lot to put on one person.

I sketch out a schedule to propose to my parents first, and then I call my mom. She's on board, so I hold onto my schedule to propose it to Sam after she gets off work tonight but before her event with Lincoln.

I spend the day taking notes on everything I'll need to cover at training camp. Before I know it, my day comes to an end and it's time to head home. Sam's in the kitchen when I walk in.

"How was work?" I ask as I set my bag on the counter and open the fridge to grab something cold to drink.

"Exhausting," she says. "And now this appearance tonight…I feel like I'm constantly on the go lately."

"I feel that," I say, and now I'm starting to feel even more guilty about what I need to ask her. "Do you think we should push forward with the break-up?"

"Probably," she says on a sigh. "I just didn't realize how taxing all the lies were going to be. It's bigger than us, you know? It's Cade. It's Devin. He's a celebrity, so it's all of Vegas, and football fans, and the world."

"Speaking of Devin—" I start, and she cuts me off with a look.

"Let's not speak of Devin please," she begs.

"Okay, okay," I say, holding up both hands placatingly. "But the offer is on the table."

"Look, Lincoln hit the nail on the head, okay? I still love him. I think I might always love him. But what would I say to him? Hi, I know we have a kid together and you just got engaged, but let's give it another go." She shakes her head. "I haven't been willing to bring it up in the five-plus years since we ended things. Why would I do it now that he's happy?"

"Because the stakes have never been higher." I sort of say it like a question even though it's not. "You need to make your feelings known before he gets married and it's too late."

"Or I sweep them under the rug because he's happy and I shouldn't come between him and his fiancée."

She's got a point.

"I just want you to be happy," I say.

GAME PLAY

"I know you do. And I love you and appreciate you. I just don't have the courage to take the risk, so I'll leave things where they are." She shrugs, but I can tell this is affecting her.

I guess I'm not one to be talking about courage given the fact that I'm secretly sleeping with my family's nemesis.

I walk over and give her a hug. "I'm sorry I've been such a bad friend that we haven't talked about this until now."

"I've been good about hiding my feelings, but since he got engaged, it's just been…hard." She sniffles, and I squeeze her tighter.

"I'm here for the easy stuff and for the hard stuff, babe."

"I know you are. And right back at you. Now I need to go get ready." She pulls back and wipes her face.

"What's tonight's event?" I ask.

"Some nightclub appearance. We have to look like we're having a good time, take some pictures, and then head out. Is Jonah with Jeremy this weekend?"

"Shockingly, yes. He said Alyssa came back and they're taking the kids to a waterpark and an aquarium this weekend."

"She came back?" she asks.

I nod.

"Dummy," she mutters, and I can't help but laugh even though I can't really argue with her on that front.

"I'm just glad Jonah might have some fun over there for a change."

"That's good news for him. How are you handling it?" she asks.

I shrug. "I still hate letting him go over there. I still want to figure out how to cut Jeremy out of our lives completely. But if he's going to make the effort, then I'm happy for

Jonah. It's the disappointment on his face every time his father lets him down that really kills me."

"Yeah, I get that," Sam says. It's a different situation entirely since Cade has a great dad in Devin, and I think what kills Sam is the split household when it should be one.

"I found out today I was approved to travel with the Aces to their training camp," I blurt.

Her jaw drops. "For the whole two weeks?"

I nod.

"Oh my God!" she squeals, and that's the reaction I was hoping for.

That's the cheering I needed from my best friend, and a pulse of relief filters through me.

She rushes toward me and pulls me into a giant hug. "I'm so happy for you!" she says when she lets me go. "What can I do?"

"I'll need help with Jonah," I admit. "I can send him to my mom and dad's house if it's easier, but—"

"Stop it. He's already here, and he and Cade are on the same schedule anyway. If he wants to go over there, that's totally fine. But I'm happy to help."

I reach over and squeeze her hand. "You are really the best friend in the entire world."

She chuckles and shoots me a grin. "I know."

Lincoln arrives, and they go to their event. They get into another public argument, and Lincoln spends the night with me at Sam's place since Jonah is at his dad's house.

The next week is a repeat of the same thing except for spending the night together. They go to another event and get into another argument.

Time marches forward, and things just keep getting harder and harder. Marcus is still in Florida but sends

GAME PLAY

communication via email and a weekly zoom call. His mom just had her surgery, and he's going to be there a few more weeks at least. Rivera is mostly staying out of my hair because he's busy managing the entire sports crew…or because he's busy planning something, and I'm nervous about what that might be.

Lincoln and I sneak in moments when we can, we record the podcast, we either go to a restaurant or do some charity work, and we suddenly find ourselves at the last weekend before training camp starts for rookies. He and Sam have another appearance tonight, and I'm feeling particularly down about it.

Lincoln shows up about forty-five minutes before they need to head out, and Sam is still getting ready when I open the door.

He ushers me into my bedroom after I let him in, and his mouth crushes down to mine before I barely even get the word *hello* out of my mouth.

His tongue batters mine as if he's a starved man searching for his next meal, and suddenly I want to *be* the meal.

He must be thinking the same thing because he abruptly stops what he's doing. He grabs me into his arms then tosses me on the bed, and he climbs up, settling back onto his knees as he unbuttons my jeans then removes them along with my panties. I sit up and start to unbutton his shirt, my fingers working furiously, and he reaches down and pulls my shirt off then unhooks my bra. I'm naked in record time, and he's still wearing far too many clothes.

He unbuckles his belt as I work his shirt, and once I get to the last button, he stands and pulls it off, tossing it on top of my clothes before he yanks his pants and boxers off.

He's naked, too, and he climbs over me. He hovers there, his cock heavy between my legs as he teases me. He drops his mouth to mine, and I feel his heat over me. He starts to move down my body, trailing kisses in his wake. He stops to suck my nipple into his mouth, and he settles there for a few beats before he trails down, down, down.

He moves his head between my legs, parting my legs wider with his palms, and he presses kisses to my inner thigh before he moves over to my hip. I shiver with anticipation, but as much as I want this, want *him*, there's something else I want even more.

"I want to taste you," I murmur from where I lay on the bed.

He freezes in his slow pursuit of my pussy, and when his eyes meet mine, there's a wicked gleam there in his. God, he's gorgeous, and I can see the lust there on his face. A needy ache presses between my thighs, and I grab one of my nipples between my fingers.

"Let me suck your dick," I say, and the words surprise even me as his eyes widen with excitement.

He presses a soft kiss to the outside of my pussy, and then he shifts so he's facing the opposite direction as me. I watch his beautiful abs as they shimmer right above my face, and then he poises his cock so it's right above me. I grab it in both fists, and he grunts as I start to stroke the head while I lower my other hand to cup his balls.

"Jesus," he mutters, and then I feel the first flick of his tongue as it makes contact with my clit. My back arches up toward his mouth as I pump his cock a few times, and then I open my mouth and take him in as deep as I can.

GAME PLAY

He starts to work his hips so he's fucking my mouth, and I keep one fist around the base of his cock while I continue to cup his balls in my other hand.

He growls as he pumps into my mouth, and the growl hums against my pussy that's growing wetter and needier by the second.

His tongue dips inside me before he moves back to my clit. He slips two fingers inside me as he continues to drive his cock in and out of my mouth. I cry out as my fist pumps up and down his shaft with each of his drives, and the vibration of my moans only pulse stronger grunts out of him. It's a push and pull between us, both of us teetering on the edge of something beautiful as he sucks and nips at my clit, his tongue pressing down and speeding up in a perfect rhythm. It takes everything in me not to fall apart. He knows what I want, and he's giving it to me even as he takes what he wants from my mouth, too. It's hot, and it's illicit, and all I can think about is exploding in a violent climax but not wanting this onslaught of pleasure to ever stop.

His licks and sucks turn nearly frantic as he tries to focus on my pleasure, and I'm doing the same to him from below as I take him in and fight against the need to come. I start to suck harder on him as he keeps thrusting into my mouth, and I feel his balls start to draw up just as he hits that magical spot inside me.

I give into the desperate need I feel, and my body falls apart. I keep sucking him as I squeeze my hand around the base of his cock. I arch into him, and that's when he starts to come, too. He lets out a ferocious roar as I feel the hot streams of come ooze out of him and hit the back of my throat. I swallow with his cock still inside my mouth as we both come at the same time. My hips jerk up to meet his glorious tongue, and he pulls some of those beautiful inches out of my mouth to give me space to breathe again.

He pumps into my mouth a few more times just as my body starts to calm, and then he moves off me and turns around, collapsing beside me with one arm draped over my stomach. He lifts a hand to rest it on my breast.

"I'm sorry," he murmurs.

"For what?"

"For not giving you some warning. But fuck, Jo, between how good your cunt tastes and hearing those moans and fucking your mouth, it snuck up on me." He sounds a little sheepish even as he talks quietly.

"I knew it was coming, and I wouldn't have wanted a warning," I admit. "I love that we're so in sync that our bodies let go at the same time."

He squeezes my breast under his palm. "I love you."

I breathe out a satisfied sigh before I say it back to him.

We lay together for another few minutes before he finally shifts a little. "I need to leave soon. You got any mouthwash?"

I giggle as I nod toward the bathroom. "Help yourself."

He forces himself up out of my bed, and goosebumps immediately rise up on my skin from the chill he leaves in his wake.

Only, I don't think it's because I'm cold. I think it has more to do with the fact that he's leaving so he can take another woman that isn't me out for the evening.

I'm supposed to be okay with this. It was partially my idea, after all. I agreed to it.

But it still stings every damn time, and I'm not sure how we ever move past this phase of our relationship and onto the next one.

CHAPTER 25

Jolene

Pictures of the happy couple make their way to the internet quickly. It's an appearance, so anyone who's there is snapping photos and tagging Lincoln on social media. Given my profession, I don't even have to do research to find them.

I study the first one I come across. They're both smiling, but neither smile quite reaches their eyes in a way that tells me they're happy together. Plenty of other people will study these photos, and some will be experts in body language. Frankly, I'm surprised they haven't been called out yet for their interactions with each other given how they look together.

Maybe it's the perfect way to transition to the break-up since they already look like they're sort of uncomfortable together.

But I know people like Rivera are studying their every move, and it's only a matter of time before someone starts up the rumor mill.

Which tells me we need to get a move on with this break-up.

I study the way Sam is leaning a bit away from him. She told me not so long ago that she was exhausted and that faking this has been hard on her. I see it in her face, in her eyes, in her fake smile.

I study Lincoln next. Handsome as always, of course, because it's Lincoln, but not quite as happy as a guy who just got his dream job should be if he's strutting around town with his supposed dream girl on his arm.

Neither one is quite the actor they think they are.

They're only gone a couple hours, and they're both quiet when they walk through the front door. I glance up from the article I'm reviewing. After studying them in detail, I threw myself into work so I wasn't focusing on the fact that it's yet another event I didn't get to attend with Lincoln.

"Anything exciting happen?" I ask.

They're both subdued when Sam says, "We played up the couple in an argument act again at the end."

"We agreed on the way home our end game should be in the next week or so," Lincoln adds. "I don't think this is working for either of us anymore, so we just need to plan how we're going to do it."

"Publicly?" I ask. "Or could you just issue a private statement in the next couple days saying the typical, you know, we've decided to part ways but will remain friends and we'd appreciate privacy during this difficult time thing?"

"Something like that," Sam murmurs. "I want to tell Cade first, of course."

"Of course." I nod. He should hear it from his mom before one of his friends hears it from his parents or social media or whatever.

"You ready?" he asks me.

GAME PLAY

"Let's go." I pull the hood of my sweatshirt up over my hair. We bid goodbye to Sam and he grabs my duffel bag for me before we head out to his car. Tomorrow is one of the last free Saturdays he'll have until March, so the plan is to spend all day together at his place.

I just hope it's as happy as I want it to be.

Thoughts swirl in my brain the entire ride over as I think about the things we need to discuss this weekend.

By the time we pull into his driveway, I feel a heavy weight settling between us. I'm both dreading and ready for the conversation I know we need to have.

He shuts the garage door before we get out of the car in case any photographers are around, and we sit in the car an extra beat.

"You okay?" he asks. We're both staring out the windshield at the garage wall.

"Yeah."

"Ready to go inside?"

"We probably should."

"What's wrong?" He reaches over and takes my hand in his, and he presses his lips to my knuckles.

I sigh as tears spring to my eyes. "I know there's a heavy conversation we need to have, and I'm scared about what direction it might go in."

"Yeah." I feel his breath against the back of my hand at his murmured word. "But the only way we're ever going to make any of this work is if we're open and honest with each other, right?"

I press my lips together.

"Come on," he says, and he opens his door and grabs my duffel. I follow him inside, where he pours us each a drink—

wine for me, whiskey for him, before we settle in together on his couch.

He clinks his glass to mine without a toast, and we each take a sip. I take a few more for liquid courage, and he watches me carefully.

"I hate watching you take my best friend out on dates that I should be going on," I blurt.

Welp, that's one way to just get it all out there.

"For what it's worth, I hate taking her when I wish it was you."

"How do we move past this, Linc?" I whisper.

He shakes his head. "I don't know. Will your dad ever be okay with us together?"

"No. Will yours?"

He blows out a long, heavy breath, and he takes a bolstering sip of whiskey. "No. But I'm not sure I care anymore."

I gasp, shocked he hasn't mentioned this to me yet. "What?"

He shakes his head a little, and he averts his eyes out the window behind me when he talks. "I guess I came to the realization that nothing I do will ever be good enough for him, and I'm barreling toward middle age and I've wasted half my life waiting for him to tell me he's proud of me. I can't do it anymore. I can't live my life like I'm a teenager anymore because I'm not. I'm not sure what hold he has on me, but I'm finally trying to fight my way out of it."

"He's your dad," I say softly. "Of course he has a hold on you. Just like mine has on me. I keep thinking what if we admit the truth to our families? How bad would that really be? But then I think about the dynamic we have, how my parents love Jonah with all their hearts and how much help

GAME PLAY

they give me. I keep thinking maybe we're just dramatizing all this, that it's not that big of a deal, but then I think…well, if Jonah were to eventually start dating Rivera's daughter, I'm not sure I'd be able to get on board with that. I know that's an extreme example, but for as much as I hate it, I also sort of get it. Us being together…it's the ultimate betrayal to our fathers."

His jaw slackens a little at my words, like I knocked the wind out of him and he's not quite sure how to respond to that.

"And I have guilt about that, Lincoln. I do. But it's not stopping me. I can't stop. I can't walk away." I reach over and take his hand in mine. "This is too damn important."

He leans over and brushes his lips across mine. "I feel the same way. I'm not willing to walk away, either. But I also can't keep living like this. We're balancing things on this tight rope and I'm anxious about how it's all going to come crashing down."

"So what do we do?" I ask, my voice nearly desperate.

"I have no idea. The season is about to start, and that'll change the dynamic again. But I want you by my side through all of it." His eyes are conflicted as they meet mine.

"I *will* be. I have to be because of my job."

He nods. "Which is just another added layer of trouble."

"Maybe I should step back. Give Rivera the correspondent position." The words come out of my mouth venomously, and they even seem to taste bad as I say them, but in some ways, this would be easier. It would take away half our issue, anyway.

"Don't say that," he chides.

I shrug. "Why not? It would be easier on us."

"Because I'm not sneaking around to fuck Rivera when we're at the vineyard in California."

I giggle. "So you'll be sneaking around to find time with me?"

"You bet your ass I will. You'll have your own room, and so will I."

"Do the players?" I ask.

He shakes his head. "Two to a room mostly because the place is small and intimate."

"Have you been there?"

He takes a sip of whiskey. "Not yet, but Jack has told me all about it."

"Will Jack make the trip out to California?" He'd be a great subject to interview for the kind of behind-the-scenes content Marcus is looking for.

"He may stop by for a few days, but he's got commitments here. Between Dalton Developments, his family, and now owning the team, he's a busy man."

"His family," I murmur. "I don't know how he does all this with two little kids."

"He's got an incredible wife and a stellar support team," he says dryly, referring a bit to himself, I think.

"He does, but man, those years when they're little are hard. With Jonah, I felt like I was always passing him off for work, but now that he's seven, he's a lot more self-sufficient in some ways and that makes things easier. He has opinions now and can tell me if he doesn't like something. I just feel like moms can't win. If we focus on our careers, we're bad moms for not spending enough time with our kids, but if we stay home, we're bad moms for not having something just for us."

GAME PLAY

"Such a double standard," he murmurs. "For the record, I don't think you're a bad mom. I think you've found a balance that works for you, and that's something everyone is striving for in life, mom or not."

"I'm a hot mess faking like I have things put together most days," I admit, and he chuckles.

"You are not."

I shrug and offer half a smile as if to say, yep, that pretty much sums me up. "You ever want that for yourself?"

"Being a hot mess that feels like I'm faking that I'm put together?" He shakes his head. "No. That doesn't sound at all like me. Or you."

"I mean kids," I clarify.

"Oh." He shrugs, and he looks uncomfortable for a beat. "I don't know. Do you want more?"

We've asked the question to each other once before, and neither of us had an answer. Still, I think about where I'm at now in life compared to where I was when I had Jonah. He was a happy surprise, but I was sort of just at the start of my career. I was only twenty-six when I got pregnant, and I thought I had my future nailed down with Jeremy.

How wrong I was.

And now I'm in a different sort of boat where I *don't* have my future nailed down other than in my career, but the thought of having a baby that has Lincoln's eyes and my lips and his leadership skills and my people skills makes me want things with him I probably have no business wanting.

I don't lay all that on him, though. It's a lot.

"I think if I was still twenty-six and in the kind of relationship where we were planning to keep moving forward together, it would be easy to say yes." I say the words carefully. "I love being a mom. It's the hardest, most rewarding, most frustrating, most incredible thing I've ever done."

"None of my brothers have kids," he murmurs. "I think our parents fucked us up more than we ever realized."

"It's not too late." The words are out before I get the chance to stop them.

His eyes meet mine. "Imagine the scandal that would be. New head coach knocks up family enemy team correspondent." He shakes his head a little as an ironic laugh bubbles up from his chest. "What the fuck are we doing, Jo?"

I sigh. "I feel like we keep asking that same question."

"We do, and all I know in terms of an answer is how I feel when I'm with you. My brain tells me to give it up. My brain says we'll never find a way to make this work when there is so goddamn much at stake. But my heart…" He pats his chest. "My heart wants to find a way. And he's winning."

Hot tears spring to my eyes at his words as he basically summarizes everything I feel where he's concerned.

I swipe my cheek, and he leans in and presses a soft kiss there.

"Where do you see yourself in five, ten years down the road?" I ask. I want to ask where he sees *us* down the road, but I'm too scared about what the answer might be.

He draws in a deep breath. "I don't know. My contract with the Aces is for three years, and if I'm good enough to stay here for those three years, I guess I hope I'll still be around beyond that."

"You guess?" I ask, sort of surprised at the way he worded that. I assumed he wanted to coach until he no longer could.

GAME PLAY

"I was never allowed to have any interests outside of football. If I did, they weren't nurtured. I didn't have a playroom filled with toys when I was a kid. I had a basket filled with footballs, all different colors and shapes and sizes. And I love the game. I do. It's my passion. But sometimes I wonder what else is out there, what else I might be missing out on. I got out of the game when I could no longer play, but I didn't *leave* the game. Now it's all game play and strategizing and play calls, and I love what I do. It's just…sometimes I wonder what else there is. Maybe I'd enjoy traveling more if I could, exploring cities that I'm in for more than a few nights because I'm there for a game. But instead of using my offseason for travel, I sink my teeth into work since I have nobody to travel with. Maybe I'd enjoy woodworking or training for marathons or fishing. Maybe I'd play golf with buddies instead of with other coaches or work associates. Maybe I'd nurture friendships and relationships unrelated to the game, and I'd get to keep those friends when I leave for a new city." He shrugs, and for the first time, I hear the loneliness in his voice.

I reach over and grab his hand in mine, and I'm about to say something about how he's not alone when he adds a final thought.

"Even with you, the one person who seems to really *get* me…I'm not allowed to be with you *because* of the game. And not just because my father took your father out of the game and your father drained my father of his dreams. But also because I'm the head coach and you're the reporter." He blows out a breath. "But that's life, you know? That's fate at work. I'm finally back with the person I love more than anyone else in the world, and I can't have her."

I set down my wineglass and then I climb on top of him. I wrap my arms around him and straddle him in a full body hug, and he leans over to deposit his whiskey glass on the end table beside us. He wraps his arms around me, too.

"You have me," I say softly into his neck, and he tightens his hold on me. "You have me forever, Lincoln, and if we have to hide forever just to be together, then that's what we do."

He sighs as he tightens his grip around me, and it finally dawns on me that this is it. This is what's going to make us stronger. We will fight through this haze together, and we will find a way out to the other side…together.

Someday we will find a way to be together in public, but the public doesn't matter. What matters is how we feel. What matters is allowing ourselves to explore that and nurture it, and as much as it sucks not to be able to share that with others—like Jonah, for instance—at least we're together.

And that's all that matters.

Or at least I wish it was…so I'll keep telling myself that until I start to believe it.

CHAPTER 26

lincoln

The rest of the week goes quickly, and suddenly I find myself with the rookies reporting to the Complex for the first day of their camp. The veterans will meet next Monday morning, and the entire team will board the buses to head to California for an intense two weeks as we get a feel for how we're going to gel as a team.

And somehow, I will find a way to sneak in time with Jolene.

It's beyond dangerous for both of us. I'll look like the horny idiot who can't keep it in my pants if we get caught, and she'll look like everything she's trying not to look like.

It's probably better to stay away from each other…but we'll be pressed together day in and day out since she's getting behind the scenes footage.

It's only two weeks.

We can do this.

Except I'm sure we can't.

I'd love to have her sleep over every night before we head out, but she can't. She's spending every possible second she has with her son, and I don't blame her.

For the first time, she really made me think about whether that's something I want, too.

I haven't spent a lot of time around kids, to be honest. I've run into Cade on occasion when I've been at Sam's place, but he definitely resents me. Jonah, on the other hand, makes me wonder whether I could really do this someday. There's something about seeing someone who is half Jolene that makes me love him without even knowing him.

And that's scary as fuck.

* * *

The first week of camp is just the rookies, though some of my older players stop by to offer feedback and help. Both Luke and Ben are here to lead meetings with the wide receivers and tight ends, respectively, along with the position coaches, and Jack offers feedback to the quarterback coach.

Brandon Fletcher showed up. He's not a rookie—in fact, he's been with the Aces longer than Jack Dalton was, but he doesn't want Miles Hudson showing him up. And I don't blame him. The question of who our QB1 is going to be is on everyone's mind right now, but Fletcher is showing up even though he doesn't have to right now. That tells me he's willing to put in the work to earn the title.

A few of our practice squad guys are here to help run drills, but we start the day on the field—mostly because it's hot as fuck in Vegas, and I don't want to wear out the rookies before the rest of the team heads to California next week.

GAME PLAY

It's how I'll run camp at the vineyard, too. The player's association limits our time on the field to two and a half hours a day, but I will fill up every other second of time that I can with off-field work.

We'll start the day with practice at nine. We'll break for lunch, and then we'll have a team meeting followed by breakout position meetings and individual workouts. We'll break for dinner and finish up the evening with our team installation drills where we review which plays from the playbook we'll be practicing in the morning. Players will be dismissed for the evening, and some will go to treatment while others will stay up studying the playbook and coaches will talk to players individually or to the media if necessary. And then it'll start all over again in the morning.

Some guys dread training camp. Not me. Even when I was a player, I was excited for it. It was the chance to be back with my brothers, the people who understand our love for this game like no one else. It's the chance to show what we're made of, to show how badly we want this. To earn our place.

But one of my favorite parts of camp is seeing those breakout players who put in the work in the offseason. There's always one who you think isn't going to make the fifty-three man roster, and then he surprises the shit out of everyone by playing hard and earning his place.

And I can't wait to see who that's going to be this year. I can't wait to see the vibe we have as I let Brandon take the helm and fight it out with Miles. Brandon's been around longer, but that doesn't mean he deserves it.

Nobody here deserves it. Not until they prove they do.

And *that* is the crux of what training camp means to me.

Jolene is here taking footage, and we pre-recorded some extra podcast segments to get us through the next few weeks since we weren't sure whether we'd have time to record while we're at the vineyard. I have no idea what it'll look like since I'm with a new team that has different needs than my old team did.

But I do know that while I'm handing a lot of responsibility over to Mike and Andy, I'll still be busy overseeing everything as I give players individual feedback and search for ways to help them improve.

The week passes quickly, and Jolene and I manage to record a few segments to send to Rivera.

She stays late to interview me as she struggles with what to send to Rivera for the podcast and what to hold onto for her own behind the scenes footage for the public, and I suggest using the best stuff for the podcast and using her broadcasts to tease it.

She loves the idea, and she thanks me for it with a quick fuck on top of my desk late at night after everyone's gone home.

I may be exhausted from the day, but I manage to find the energy to pump into her until we both come.

Before I know it, it's Monday morning and we're meeting at the bus lot.

I invited Megan to come along—mostly because she's become a valuable asset to me, inputting all my scribbled notes that I take on the field and editing the playbook as needed, which has been fairly often so far.

The thing I think I like most about her is that I didn't even have to train her. She offers to do things for me I didn't even know she knew how to do because they are things Coach Thompson had her do, and if it takes something off my already full plate, I'm jumping at it.

GAME PLAY

I spot Jolene in the bus lot as she watches players bid their families goodbye, and I can't help but wonder how hard it was for her to leave her son this morning. He isn't here saying goodbye, and neither is Sam—my girlfriend for all intents and purposes.

We haven't officially *broken up* yet. We figured we'll be apart anyway, so it doesn't really matter. But once the season gets underway, we'll issue a statement like the one Jolene suggested the other day.

The players bid their families goodbye, and there's nobody for me to say goodbye to, so I get on the bus. I should feel a stab of loneliness at that, but I don't. I can't when the only person I'd want to say goodbye to is coming with us.

She steps on the bus shortly after I do, and she glances around. "Can we sit anywhere?" she asks, and I nod.

She takes the seat across from me.

It's not a short drive to get to California, and Megan told me Coach Thompson used to fly in. But I'm not Mitch. I want to experience this with my team. I coach from the trenches.

Players start to board the bus, and I grimace a little when Austin Graham steps on. That grimace turns to a full glare when he slides into the seat beside Jolene.

They start to talk, and I force the jealous feelings away. I force those familiar feelings of loneliness away, too.

I know where her heart is.

But that doesn't mean I like it…and it doesn't mean I have to give Graham any playing time at all. In fact, as I watch my brother step onto the bus next, I have a feeling Graham will be seeing much more of the pine this year than he was expecting to.

And as Jolene tosses her head back with a laugh and I slip in my earbuds to listen to a podcast, wishing I'd booked a flight instead of riding this dumb bus, I can't help but think I don't really feel so bad for Graham.

CHAPTER 27

Jolene

Me: Relax, Coach. You know I'm just being nice.

He glances up to see Austin is no longer sitting beside me, and the pinch between his brows seems to smooth over. I laugh a little at his reaction, and he taps on his phone. My phone buzzes with his text a beat later, and it's a little funny that we're texting each other when we're sitting a few feet apart, but I'm not sure how else we can communicate.

Before I get a chance to read his text, I watch as his secretary, Megan, slides into the seat with him.

My claws come out, and I guess I get why he doesn't like when Austin is friendly with me. He flips his phone over so she can't see it, and I read his text to me.

Lincoln: I'll show you nice when I bend you over my bed and make you see stars.

Dear Lord.

Well, now I see why he hid his phone. I don't care that Megan is sitting with him. I text him anyway. He'll read it when he can.

Me: Is that a threat or a promise?

His eyes shift to me so he knows the origin of the buzzing of his phone, but he doesn't check it while he chats with Megan. I'd love to know what they're talking about, exactly, but their voices are low and I can't hear them.

I did have a nice conversation with Austin, though. He asked how Jonah is doing and raved about my son's talent, so of course I enjoyed the chance to brag on my boy, especially since I miss him already.

Lincoln kept shooting us dirty looks until finally he turned to face out the window, and now I find myself doing the same thing.

How different would this be if we could share our secret?

My guess is very different. The team wouldn't have invited me along, for one thing. Having a significant other at training camp would prove to be nothing more than a distraction, but I'm vowing here and now not to get in his way.

We finally arrive at the vineyard, and it's a lovely place out in the middle of virtually nowhere. The team rents out the entire facility for two weeks, and there are several practice fields and plenty of space to hold these first two weeks of camp as these men start to work together as a team for the first time.

Before we boarded the bus, Lily was in the parking lot handing out keys, so we all head straight to our rooms upon arrival. I'm in a room all by myself, and I'm not sure if Lincoln purposely arranged it or not, but my room is adjacent to his—as I find out when we both stop in front of our doors at the same time.

GAME PLAY

I glance over at him with a sly smile before I head inside, and when I get in there, I find that there's a door connecting our two rooms.

He had to have arranged it. It's just too big a coincidence that we'll be able to actually spend time together undetected over the next two weeks. I open the door the same time he does, and we meet in the middle as our bodies smash together and our lips collide.

He kisses me like it's his oxygen, like this kiss is giving him sustenance, and I'm just about to lose myself in it when he pulls his mouth from mine, but he doesn't let me go quite yet.

"Oh, this is going to work out very nicely."

"How'd you manage this?" I ask.

He chuckles. "Purely coincidence. All the single rooms are on this floor, and only a handful of us have them. Close the door every time you leave, but when you're here, keep it open," he demands. "I'll join you when I can."

"Are you sure? I don't want either of us to get caught."

"We won't." Even as he says the words, there's a knock at his door. He draws a single finger up to his lips as if to tell me to be quiet, and then he closes the door on his side separating the two of us. I glance around the room and set to unpacking the essentials before I head over to the window to check out the view. Virtually everyone is in their own rooms right now, but a handful of players are already outside exploring the grounds. I don't want to get in anybody's way just yet, and I know there's a team meeting in another hour, so I decide to just chill in my room for a bit—to decompress after the bus ride and let everyone get acclimated before I start bombarding them with questions.

I'm not invited to all the events. I can't attend team meetings because of privacy issues, and I can't go to full practices every day—just an hour of practice every other day. But I can be in the open areas and I can hang out in the cafeteria and on the grounds. I can talk to players in the fitness rooms but not the training room, and I can hold office hours for coach and player interviews, and it's way more access than my counterparts at other news channels have.

And it's all thanks to Ellie and the podcast. It was a way to capitalize on the community events, and given that the team owner is her brother-in-law, it was an easy enough sell for her to get me here.

I'm so incredibly thankful, and for that, I shoot Ellie a quick text thanking her. I put my shoes back on and decide to head downstairs for a walk and to see what players do when first arriving at camp, but just as I'm leaving my room, I see Megan coming out of the room next door.

She's patting down her hair and smoothing down her shirt, and if I don't know better, I'd think she just had a romp with Coach Nash.

If I didn't know better, I'd be concerned about the little smile playing at her lips that look red and swollen.

And even though I do know better, a jealous rage still fills me.

It's the hot temper rearing its ugly head, and I've managed to keep it in check since things have been going well between us, but I'm not going to stand by and wonder. The miscommunication and assumption thing might work for other people, but it damn well doesn't work for me.

"Oh, hey," Megan says as she passes by me.

GAME PLAY

"Hi." I turn to look back at my door. "Oh, shit. Forgot something." I'm muttering to myself but loud enough that she hears me, and I head back into my room.

I open the door separating my room from Lincoln's and I start banging on his.

It opens a few seconds later. "Why are you banging on the door?" he asks calmly, as if Megan wasn't just leaving his room looking all nice and freshly fucked.

Hold it together, Bailey.

"What was Megan doing in here?" I demand.

He looks confused for a beat before he glances at the door she just walked through.

"She's my assistant," he says. "She was checking in to see if there's anything I need."

"And you needed her out of her shirt?" I demand.

"What the hell are you talking about?"

"She just walked out of your room patting down her hair and smoothing out her shirt wearing a smile like she was freshly fucked and satisfied."

"Excuse me?" he asks, clearly confused, and his confusion makes me feel a little better but my temper has now taken hold.

"Oh don't play dumb." I roll my eyes.

He takes a menacing step toward me, and I think he expects me to back up, but I don't. I stand firm.

His eyes heat over. "Jealousy is hotter on you than I imagined it would be."

"What's going on between you two?" I hiss.

He takes another step and runs the back of his fingers down my cheek. "Were you imagining her riding on top of me or underneath me?"

My jaw clenches tightly as fire lights in my eyes. "Neither. I was imagining you being faithful to me because of the things we've said."

"We didn't make any promises," he argues.

And he's right, we didn't. But that doesn't stop my hand from coming up to connect with his cheek.

He doesn't look surprised that I just slapped him. He doesn't move or react. It's as if it didn't faze him in any way at all, which only serves to heighten my anger.

"What did you do with her?" I hiss through that clenched jaw of mine.

His brows arch, and then he shakes his head. "I didn't touch her. I imagine she saw you in the hallway as she left my room and wanted to get a rise out of you, Jolene. And clearly…it worked. It's not like she hasn't heard us in my office on more than one occasion. The only time I shut my door is when you visit."

I take a step away from him as embarrassment sets in, but he links an arm around my waist and hauls me into him, clearly not about to let me get away with anything.

"I have two things I need to say to you. One, I have work to do while I'm here, and I need to focus. I have neither the time nor the inclination to cater to these ridiculous accusations. And two, you are mine. I am yours. There is no one else. We might not have made any promises, but I vow that to you here and now. But if you can't control your temper, and if you ever think of raising a hand to me again, I will send you back to Vegas so fast your head will spin. Understood?"

My nostrils flare in anger, but he's absolutely right—no matter how much I don't want to admit it.

GAME PLAY

I try to back out of his hold, but he's got me locked in tightly against his body.

I blow out a frustrated breath. "Fine. Understood."

His mouth quirks a little in a sort of half-smile. "Great." He reaches a hand down and cups my pussy outside my jeans. "Now as much as I want to punish you for even thinking I'd look at another woman," he says as he drives that hard erection toward my hips to prove how much that's true, "I need to get downstairs to meet with the coaching staff." He flicks open the button of my jeans then reaches his hand down until he slides his finger right into my pussy. "Stay the fuck out of trouble while I'm gone," he says, and I let out a soft moan as he pumps his finger in and out of me, "and be here tonight at midnight for that punishment."

My entire body throbs at the mere thought of being punished by this man as he continues driving his finger in and out of me. My hips sway to meet each drive of his finger, my body betraying me since I want to be mad. But I can't be when he's doing this to me, and the pure pleasure takes over my every thought as the need to climax pulses through me.

My moans get louder as I get closer. And then…it all stops. He pulls his hand out of my jeans and buttons them back up.

"Don't you dare finish that without me." He sounds angry as he says it.

Holy shit.

So that's the punishment.

Or…at least that's part of it.

My pussy aches with need at the mere anticipation of it.

I lean forward to kiss him, to seal what just happened between us into some sort of promise, but he lets me go and backs away. He grabs his tablet and walks out of his room, leaving me standing there a panting, needy hot mess who really needs to get downstairs to interview players with this need to come sitting heavy between my thighs.

CHAPTER 28
lincoln

I'm antsy as I wait for this meeting to come to an end. The first day of camp is usually nothing more than arrival day, but since we're starting with practice tomorrow morning, we're having a team meeting where I go over the plays we'll practice in the morning. I'm going to hit them with the long drive drill tomorrow, which means we'll start on the five-yard line on one end of the field and reset with a different play every five yards all the way down the field. That's eighteen plays, and it'll show me who's been busy memorizing the playbook and who's been fucking around.

I give them twenty-five plays to focus on, not telling them which eighteen I'll run, and the entire coaching staff is ready to see what these players can do tomorrow morning.

The evening finally comes to an end, and I recap with Mike and Andy with a drink at the bar before I head up to my room.

It's a little after midnight, and I'm exhausted…but not too exhausted to make good on my word to Jolene earlier.

I thought she knew where we stood. I thought she trusted me.

But it's clear to me now that she doesn't. And tonight, I'm going to make damn sure to show her.

The door between our rooms on my side is closed, and I don't bother warning her with a text. Instead, I open my side, and hers is open.

She's laying on her bed watching television. The lights are off. The curtains are drawn.

She looks sweet and innocent there as she waits for me, and the things I have planned are the opposite. I want to corrupt and debase her.

"Hi," she says softly.

I don't say a word back.

My heart races as I close the door between our rooms, and she flicks off the television, casting us in darkness.

Even from where I stand, her breathing quickens, and my dick pulses painfully in my black pants as it begs for escape.

I don't say a word as I move toward the bed. It's too dark in here, but maybe that makes what's about to go down even sexier.

I'll admit I spent part of my evening imagining what I was going to do to her while Mike talked offense and Andy talked defense. I imagined shoving my cock down her throat. I imagined fucking her tits. I imagined taking her to the edge then pulling back, withholding her orgasm even longer as punishment.

"I want you naked. Now," I demand.

I strip out of my clothes as I see shadows of movement in the dark room. There's a little gap in the curtains, allowing a bit of moonlight to cast a glow as my eyes adjust to the darkness.

GAME PLAY

My mind runs wild with possibilities, but as my mouth waters, I know where I'm going to start.

And I dive right in without warning, burying my tongue in her hot cunt.

"Oh," she gasps, and her hands move to my head, threading through my hair.

She's so goddamn wet for me, ready as she waited like a good girl, and I want to lead her to climax, but I also want to stretch this out.

I nip and suck at her clit before dipping my tongue down into that sweet cunt again, and her hips start to buck as she rides my face.

I can tell she's getting close as her body starts to tighten beneath my touch, and that's when I pull back.

"Not yet," I say, and she cries out with a strangled, frustrated sob. I start to move along her body until I find her tits and I straddle her there, push them together, and slide my dick through the valley between them.

She reaches down and puts her hands over mine, and I let go so I can roll and pinch her nipples as I fuck her tits—something I've wanted to do since we were teenagers, if I'm being honest.

And it's every bit as hot as I thought it would be.

She moves a hand from where she's cupping the side of one of her breasts, and I put my hand back. She reaches for the head of my cock as it slides between her tits, and she starts to stroke me as I move.

She moves her other hand, and I'm forced to stop touching her nipple to hold her breast in place. She reaches down and cups my balls in her other hand as she keeps stroking the tip, and as much as I'd planned on fucking both her mouth and her pussy tonight, it's too many sensations at once. We'll have time for those another day. Tonight, this is how I'm coming.

I let out a loud grunt as my balls tighten and I start to come, and I bat her hands out of the way so I can let go all over those gorgeous tits. I growl as I stroke my cock, jets of come streaming out of the head and onto her body, and I wish there was more light in here so I could see the masterpiece that is me claiming that sweet, sweet body of hers.

As soon as I'm done, I flick on the light on the nightstand beside us.

"Hey!" she says, shielding her eyes as she squints in the dark, and I sit up between her legs to admire how fucking hot she looks with my come all over those perfect, gorgeous tits.

It's nearly enough to make me come again, but I'm fucking spent.

"Well, thanks. Goodnight," I say, and I climb off the bed as I start to head toward my room.

"What?" she balks.

I halt where I am. I was never really planning to leave—not without making her come first, of course, and I *am* a fucking gentleman so I'll at least get her a washcloth since there's semen all over her tits.

"What?" I ask.

"What about…you know…"

"Say it, Jolene," I demand.

"I want to…you know. You said I should wait, and I did, and I need to." The needy desperation in her voice is hot as fuck.

"Need to what?" I ask.

"Come," she whispers.

GAME PLAY

I blow out a breath. "Ask like you mean it."

"Will you please give me a fucking orgasm before I die over here?" she blurts, and I can't help my laugh.

I head to the bathroom first to make her wait just a little longer, and I return with a washcloth. I wipe my jizz off her chest, and then I move down between her legs. I shove my tongue back into her pussy, and I drop a finger a little lower down into the tight bud of her ass. She squeals when I do it, and I move my tongue up to her clit as I insert a finger from my other hand into her pussy.

"Oh, God, oh my God!" she practically screams, and I know we need to be quiet since we're in a hotel with the rest of my team, but I fucking love hearing how much she appreciates what I'm doing to her.

She comes nearly immediately and violently, her body tensing and pulsing over and over as I keep both fingers inside her, my tongue pressing to her clit until the waves crest and she starts to come back down from the high. It's so intense, so hot, so gorgeous that I feel nearly ready to go again, to get inside that pussy and fuck her for the rest of the night.

But we're both spent. Exhausted. Sated.

She's panting, and I watch her beautiful face as she starts to cry.

Oh fuck.

Did I hurt her?

"What's wrong?" I murmur softly as I stroke her hair and press a soft kiss to her temple.

"Holy shit, Lincoln," she whispers through her tears. "That was incredible. I've never come that hard before."

I lean down and press a kiss to her lips, the first time I've kissed her tonight. "I hope you know what you mean to me after that. There is nobody else. Only you. You own me. So get ready for a lifetime of climaxes like that, Jo."

Even as the words leave my mouth, though, I fear they're just lip service. I don't know if we have a lifetime.

And the mere thought of that nearly makes *me* start to cry, too.

CHAPTER 29
Jolene

He holds me through the night, and he slips back to his room early in the morning so he can prepare for his day.

It was an intense night, one fraught with feelings and words, and I feel secure in what we have.

Only...I'm not sure how secure it is when we're sneaking around.

We weren't exactly quiet last night, but I also don't see anyone confronting either of us about it. Nobody is going to ask the coach if he was having sex last night, and equally, nobody is going to ask the reporter if she was busy getting down last night.

So we're professional when we're not alone, but when it's just the two of us, we can celebrate what we've found together.

His words from last night play on repeat in my mind.

You own me.

Get ready for a lifetime.

I wish we could get ready for a lifetime together, but we're teetering on this bridge and I'm starting to fear that the only way down is a crash landing.

The two weeks in California pass in the blink of an eye. I spend my days when I'm not interviewing players or coaches either drafting stories or taking notes for podcast material and story material for VG-oh-three, I spend my evenings video chatting with my son, and I spend my nights wrapped in the coach's arms.

He usually slips in when I'm already asleep and he's gone before I wake, and we were only intimate that one time the first night here, but it seems like we did a fairly good job of hiding what's really going on between the two of us.

Or so I thought.

We're boarding the bus back home, and Austin slides into the seat beside me again.

"How was your time at our training camp?" he asks. He's being friendly, and he's one of the players who has been the easiest to interview over the last two weeks.

"Great. Yours?"

"Exhausting." He nods out the window at the vineyard we're about to leave. "But you saw it all go down. Did you get some good footage?"

I nod. "And excellent interviews." I tap my laptop sitting conveniently on my lap, and he smiles.

Once the bus is in motion, he turns the conversation from small talk to something else.

"I like you, Jolene," he begins. "And that's why I wanted to tell you about the rumors going around about you."

My brows dip together. "Rumors?"

He clears his throat. "People are saying you and the coach are a thing."

GAME PLAY

"Me? And Lincoln?" I make a *pfft* sound as if that's the most ridiculous notion anyone has ever said. "You know our families are basically enemies, right?"

"Yeah, that's the story, and that's why people think you're both being so secretive about it."

I shake my head even as my heart races that we've been outed. Caught. "It's been ingrained in me my entire life to hate him and his family," I say, keeping my voice low. "Besides, why would I risk my career on something like that?"

"How would it be risking your career?"

"My integrity, for one thing. People already assume I got this job by sleeping my way there, which I most certainly did not. But could you imagine the scandal if it broke that we were an item?" I make a face and shake my head. "No thanks. Add on top of that how focused he is on the season and the team and doesn't need these rumors abounding, never mind the fact that he's actually already in a relationship with *my roommate*, and I'd just really appreciate if you could put a stop to those rumors when you hear them."

"Right." He nods, and he clears his throat. "I'd probably be inclined to believe you despite the defensive tone, but the truth is…your curtains were open this morning, and a few of us saw him in your room."

"Yeah, because his hot water went out." I roll my eyes. "It's nothing more, Austin." I say the words quietly, forcefully, urgently.

He nods. "Okay. Then go on a date with me."

"Oh, Austin, that's really sweet, but—"

He tilts his head and interrupts me. "But."

I sigh. The only way he's going to believe me is if I accept, and I suppose one date with a player is less egregious than dating the coach. At least nobody will assume I got the job because of a second-string tight end. I'll spend the night talking about my son and the six-year age difference between Austin and me to scare him off, and things will be fine.

"Fine. I'd love to." I offer a tight smile.

"Great. I'm free tonight. Are you?"

"I haven't seen my son in two weeks, so I'm planning to spend the weekend with him."

"How about lunch on Monday?" he presses.

I haven't been in the office in two weeks, but I'll consider this a working lunch, I guess. "Sure."

We figure out a place and time before he heads toward the back of the bus, and there's a text from Lincoln waiting for me when I glance at my phone.

Lincoln: *What was that all about?*

I glance over at him, and he looks irritated as his eyes find mine.

He taps something out on his phone, and I glance down when mine dings with a text notification.

Lincoln: *I meant what I said. You are mine. I am yours.*

Me: *I know. He said there are rumors going around that you and me are a thing. He saw you in my room this morning. I made up a story about how you didn't have hot water and then he asked me on a date to prove I'm not seeing you.*

Lincoln: *What the fuck? What did you say?*

Me: *I didn't have a choice if I wanted him to believe my story. I accepted.*

His eyes are livid when they meet mine. He doesn't write back, and it's a long six hours back to Vegas.

And admittedly, I spend the remainder of the trip wondering whether he's got another one of those terribly erotic punishments in store for me.

CHAPTER 30
Jolene

I spend the weekend with Jonah, and it feels so good to be back home again. I continue to wish that we could find a way to mesh these two parts of my life—that I could wake in Lincoln's arms then spend the day with my son, but right now, it's just not possible.

Lincoln worked all weekend, and we've barely spoken at all since the bus ride when he was clearly upset that I'm going on a date with a player on his team. He hasn't brought it up, but I still can't help wondering whether he's taking it out on Austin. I've asked him about a hundred times who will be the starting quarterback as I try to find some angle to persuade him to tell me, but I'm almost positive he hasn't decided yet. He wants to see both Brandon and Miles in action at the preseason games, and then he'll decide.

When I walk into the restaurant we agreed on, Austin is already there. He waves me over, and I feel a little nervous going out in public with a player, but it's too late to turn back now.

"Hey," he says, and he stands to greet me with a kiss on the cheek.

"How's your Monday going?" I ask as I sit in the chair across from him.

"Better now." He offers a smile, and he's very cute. He's a little young for me, but the dark hair that swoops down over his forehead and those blue eyes are just enough to make me forget about our ages.

But there's one little detail I heard about him that I'm not as comfortable with, and that's the fact that he's a member of a sex club.

Or he was, at least.

The story broke in the gossip rags last year at training camp, but the excitement around it has long since tapered. It's no longer a *secret* club, though it's certainly private, and it wasn't a *sex club*, exactly—while sex happened on the top floor, it was more of an exclusive club for celebrities. I've since learned that there were once four owners, but the other owners sold their stakes to Victor Bancroft since he was the only one comfortable with the secret getting out. The other owners' identities were always shrouded in secrecy, and as much as I wanted to know more, I've since let it go. It's old news now, anyway, but it did give the regular, average joe a look into the private lives of celebrities when it hit newsstands.

I wonder if Austin is still a member.

I want to ask, but I don't want him to think I'm interested in going.

Maybe with Lincoln, if we could. But not with Austin.

"So this is your…fourth season with the Aces?" I ask.

He nods. "Once Olson retired, I was ready to move into the starting position. But then Coach brought over his brother, and after camp, it looks like I'm going to be in the same place I've been all four years."

GAME PLAY

"You're still a key member of the team," I point out, and he shrugs.

"Yes and no," he says, and I'm curious if he still believes I'm sleeping with the coach and can put in a good word for him.

In fact, now that I've had the thought, I can't help but wonder if that's why he asked me out in the first place—combined, of course, with wanting to prove he was right when he accused me of sleeping with Lincoln.

We place our orders, and we chat about training camp and all things football. I keep trying to bring up Jonah just to prove that he's a single, young man who can have pretty much any woman he wants, so why does he want a single mom who's older than him, but every time I try to drive home that point, he brings up the camps he runs for kids.

We're getting nowhere. He's perfectly nice, but I keep trying to figure out his angle, and at this point, I'm starting to think this was a ploy to get me to promote his camps on the podcast.

I'm not really sure what he's after, and so I wait until the end of the meal after he's picked up the check to ask. "As a reporter, I've become very direct in my line of questioning and I've also become very suspicious of intentions. So I have to ask…why'd you want to take me to lunch?"

He chuckles. "Well, I didn't. If you recall, I wanted a date, preferably for dinner, but I took what you had open. I told you, Jolene. I like you. I find you incredibly attractive. You're ambitious, and you're smart, and you're funny. You seem to be a great mom to your little boy. And on top of all that, nobody would think twice about you dating a player, so it could be mutually beneficial for us both."

He's not wrong.

"That's very sweet, Austin," I say, and I reach across the table to take his hand in mine. I squeeze his. "I'm just…in a complicated place in my life right now. I don't want to get into anything."

"Is that code for letting me down gently? Or is that code for being open to a friends with benefits sort of situation?"

I laugh. "The first one. I'm sorry."

He stands and lets out a disappointed sigh. "I understand." He reaches out a hand to help me up, and he gives me a friendly hug. And then he shocks the hell out of me by planting a kiss on my lips.

"Whoa," I say, planting my hands on his chest and pushing him away.

"I'm sorry," he says a little sheepishly. "I just thought I could change your mind…"

"By kissing me without an invitation?" My brows dip together. We're in public, so I rein it in. "Thanks for lunch, Austin. I had a nice time. But I need to get back to work."

"Of course. I'm so sorry."

I turn to walk out of the restaurant, and he walks me to my car. He's gentlemanly, and the kiss back there seemed to just be a little out of character for him. It's over and done now, and I'm going to choose to leave it in the past.

Except…I can't.

As soon as I walk into the office, Rivera is at my cubicle waiting for me.

"What the fuck are these?" he asks, and he has prints of photos from my lunch with Austin.

I look through them in confusion…until I get to the last one in the pile.

The one of Austin kissing me.

GAME PLAY

Confusion turns to anger, and this feels like one big setup.

"Where did you get these?" I ask evenly.

"Someone just emailed them to me," he says, and he really looks like a little weasel perched there leaning against my desk.

"I literally just left lunch with him. Someone sent these to you already? You didn't have them taken?"

He puts on the act like he can't believe I'd suggest such a thing. "First I catch you kissing Nash, and now you're with a player? Really making the rounds there, Bailey. Wait until Marcus gets a load of these."

"Fuck off out of here, Rivera," I mutter.

"Is that how you talk to your boss?"

"No, it's not. But you're not my boss. So kindly get the fuck out before I have you removed."

He laughs. "Okay, yeah." His tone drips with sarcasm. "Have me removed then."

I lift a hand as if I'm going to slap him, and he flinches. I don't do it, but it's proof I've got him where I want him. He might be threatening me with photos, but he's still a little scared of me.

Okay, so maybe I don't have him *right* where I want him. But I like that he's a little afraid.

"Get. Out," I hiss, and he scampers off, leaving his stupid photos behind on my desk.

I toss them in the trash after ripping them up, but I'm well aware how photos work these days. Digital copies have presumably already been distributed across the interwebs, and surely my *boyfriend* is going to have a conniption fit that I was caught kissing one of his players.

I text him in order to stave off the potential consequences.

Me: *Just got back to the office after lunch. Austin tried to kiss me. I firmly pushed him away, but needed you to know before pics hit the internet.*

I feel like a colossal idiot as soon as I send the text. I'm not sure if he's stewing over it or if he's just busy, but I don't get a reply right away, so I stop staring at my phone waiting for one and dive into work.

They're already out there. All over the place. Pics of me with Austin's mouth on mine, and I know Lincoln's reaction isn't going to be pretty.

It's several hours before the reply comes.

Lincoln: *I need to see you. My house in an hour.*

I glance at the clock. I need to be home in an hour to meet the boys coming off the school bus.

Me: *Can't. Boys get home then.*

Lincoln: *Fine, then. Gridiron break room, ten minutes.*

I can't help but wonder why he wants to meet me there and not his office, but I agree.

Me: *If you're walking over and don't want anyone to see you slipping into the break room, there's a back door that'll be unlocked.*

He sends me a thumbs up, the most passive aggressive emoji in existence, and I make my way over to my dad's bar.

Lucky for me, my parents aren't in today, and deliveries are done for the day. He's sitting at the round table back there where I used to do my homework when I walk in, and he immediately stands and strides over toward me. He fists my biceps and smashes his lips to mine.

"These are my lips," he says, his breath hot against my mouth. "No one else's."

GAME PLAY

He's filled with something I've never seen from him, and it's pretty dang hot.

"If you thought I was jealous when your assistant left your room that first day at the vineyard, that had nothing on this, Coach."

He flattens his lips as he glares at me. "Why'd he kiss you?"

"I'm not sure." I shrug. "My guess is it was for the photo op. But I did my due diligence. I went out with him, and now I don't have to do it again."

"It feels bigger than that," he says, shaking his head a little as he lets me go. He paces a few steps back and forth.

"He's getting under your skin, and you're letting him," I say softly.

"You're goddamn right he is," he mutters. "I need to get rid of him. He isn't going to play for me anyway, and now this?" He shakes his head. "Forget it."

I blow out a breath. "Why isn't he going to play for you?"

"Asher is." He says it like it's the obvious answer and I should've known that.

"What if something happens to him? Who's your TE-two?"

He exhales both loudly and dramatically.

I walk over and rest my palm on his shoulder. "Look, he tried and it didn't pan out. Let him play the game. He's good, and you know that. You can't let your feelings for me keep you from doing what's best for your team."

He runs both hands through his hair, and he tugs at it a little. When he's done, the result is that his hair is sticking up. I brush it down for him with my fingertips as I press the front of my body to his.

"I'm yours," I say softly. "Never doubt that again."

He draws in a breath as if he's breathing me in. "Okay. I need to get back to the office, and you need to get home. No more dates. Understand?"

I can't help but push back to the way he just worded that. "I make my own decisions, so I'm not going to stand here and say *yes, sir*. But I will say that there is nobody else I want to be with, and you are mine as much as I am yours."

He clenches his jaw at my words, but eventually he nods. "Fine." He leans down for another quick kiss, and then he walks out the back door of the break room.

CHAPTER 31

Jolene

Games aren't broadcast on VG03, but because I'm the local team correspondent for our little station, I'm allowed on the sidelines during all home games, including preseason ones like today. I'll be in the crowd at away games, but the first pre-season game is being played at our home field against the Falcons.

I've been on the field before, but not during a game. The excitement is palpable, and nerves rack me as I get ready to watch this team that means so much to me play their first game.

All eyes will be on Lincoln as he takes the field for his first ever game as a head coach, and I can't wait to watch him in action.

I arrived early here at the stadium, and I've already interviewed several coaches, including Lincoln, and several players during warm-ups. I've talked to fans to gather their reactions, and Dave has been with me catching video all morning. We've already recorded several teasers and broadcast a couple of live segments to get our viewers excited about our home team this year.

Kickoff is at one o'clock, and in just a few minutes, teams will be introduced onto the field.

The crowd is gathering in their seats, some with beer and others with snacks, and fans are ready.

I watch as the coaching staff starts to take the sideline. My eyes are on the head coach, and he glances around the stadium for a few beats before his eyes land on mine.

His lips curl into a small, secret smile meant just for me, and I watch as a sense of calm seems to wash over him.

He's ready for this. He's nervous and excited, of course, but he's ready.

The announcer takes the microphone, and the crowd goes wild as he starts introducing the players. Everyone is here, though our starters will only take the field for a short time.

Lincoln still hasn't announced who will be our starting quarterback, and both Miles and Brandon are dressed for the game.

A rush of excitement fills me as I watch the sideline in front of me fill with players, and then the other team is announced. One national anthem and coin toss later, and it's finally time for kickoff.

The Aces get the ball first, and the Falcons kick it deep but kick returner Isaiah Taylor catches it and runs it up the field all the way into Falcon territory on the thirty-five yard line.

All eyes are on the sideline as we watch to see which quarterback will take the field, and I see Lincoln as he nods at number ten: Miles Hudson.

The crowd goes wild as we all watch with anticipation to see what this brand-new quarterback out of Northwestern

GAME PLAY

can do for this team as he steps into the shoes of the formidable JD5 himself, Mr. Jack Dalton.

Miles runs onto the field and completes his first pass and his second. The boys move up the field and he hands off to Jaxon Bryant, who rushes into the end zone to score on the first drive of the game.

The crowd goes wild.

Miles plays a few more drives before he's replaced with Brandon, who scores on his first throw, too. The Falcons are held to a field goal, and I watch the game and take notes as I report back to the studio and scribble questions to ask when I get a moment with a player or a coach. Before I know it, it's halftime, and the second half is just as fast.

The Aces end up winning by a healthy seventeen points. Coach Nash led his team to victory in his first ever game as a head coach with a new team and new leadership.

The sense of pride that bubbles up inside me is overwhelming.

The home team's fanbase goes wild, spilling out into the concourses to celebrate the first victory of the preseason as they make their way toward the exits. Even from my spot on the field, I can hear chants of excitement.

I hang around for the post-game press conference. Dave leaves, but I wait in my seat patiently in the media room as the rest of the media members clear out.

I'm the sole person remaining, and I'm still scribbling notes when the door opens and Lincoln steps in.

"Good game, Coach," I say softly.

His offers a smile. "Thanks. We made a few mistakes, but overall I'm happy with how it went."

"It's that solid playbook," I say softly.

He takes a few steps over toward me. "What are you still doing here?"

"Taking notes." I shrug. "Waiting for you."

"Oh?"

"Care to celebrate?"

He chuckles, but his eyes seem to burn with heat.

A shiver runs down my spine as he comes closer, and when he's close enough, the scent of bergamot wafts over to me.

He leans down and runs his nose along mine. "How exactly would you like to celebrate?" His voice is low and raspy, and my heart starts to race with possibilities.

"Well, I'd say we could head out and grab a drink, but considering we're seeing each other in secret, that doesn't seem to be an option."

"No, it's not," he says quietly as he shakes his head. He smirks at me. "I've got something else in mind, anyway." His lips drop to mine, and then he hauls me up out of my chair. He carries me over toward the stage where he and players on his team sat to answer questions from the media just a few minutes ago, his mouth back on mine as he reaches into my pants to shove a finger into me.

"Oh," I moan softly, and he drives that finger in and out a few times to test out how wet I am.

Soaked is the answer. It was hot watching him coach, hot watching him answer the media's questions as he saved secret glances for me, and hot that he came back here to see if I was still here. The entire night has been like foreplay between us, and here we are.

He pulls my pants down, yanking them off over one of my legs to give me room, then undoes his pants and pulls

GAME PLAY

his cock out, and he moves so quickly that my head is practically spinning as he plunges into me.

We could get caught here at any second, and the thought of it is both thrilling and intoxicating. And a little insane…but it's *why* he has to move quickly.

He drives into me hard and steady, immediately finding the rhythm our bodies have already learned so damn well, and I just lie back and enjoy the ride as I wrap my legs around his waist and he stands on the floor fucking me as I lie back on the stage.

Each thrust causes stars to pulse behind my eyes, and my body starts to tighten as his deep strokes fill me over and over again. My pussy starts to clench around him as he moves, and I let go, giving into the pleasure and the feel and the illicitness as it all overwhelms me at once.

He lets out a growl as he feels my pussy tightening over and over on his cock, and he lets go, too, filling me with every last drop he has as we celebrate his amazing victory on the field tonight in the media room.

Just as he finishes inside me, we hear noises outside the room we're in.

"Shit," he mutters, and he pulls quickly out of me as he shoves his cock back into his pants and zips up while I scramble to get my pants back on and pulled up as fast as I can.

Just as we're finishing putting ourselves back together, the door opens.

"There you are," Jack says to Lincoln, and dear Lord, that was a close call. Literally *seconds* earlier, and we would've been caught. Steve is right behind Jack, and they both walk up to Lincoln to offer their congratulations.

Jack glances at me. "So sorry if we interrupted an interview, Ms. Bailey," he says. "But we've got to take the coach out for a celebration."

"No worries. I'll catch up with you soon, Coach," I say, and I offer a smile even though my heart is beating about a million miles a minute right now.

Holy hell.

That was a close one.

We have got to be more careful…only, when the attraction pulls as strongly between two people as it does with Lincoln and me, I'm not sure we can help ourselves.

I've never been in a relationship like that before—one where I just want to tear his clothes off all the time, where I just want him inside me, fucking me, all day every day.

And here we are, now months into a secret relationship that was over two decades in the making, and that fire hasn't started to fade at all while we've built on the emotional side of our relationship, too.

I'm just not sure how many more close encounters my heart can take.

CHAPTER 32
lincoln

Yeah, we won our first preseason game. But mistakes were made, as I said to Jolene, and now we course correct so we don't make them again next week.

Most players have Monday off since we won. But those who racked up penalties each have appointments with me today to go over film and discuss what happened.

First up bright and early at nine in the morning is my very own little brother.

"Coach, Asher's here," Megan says when she calls into my office. She never mentioned what went down with Jolene, but I have to think she did it on purpose. She's been her consistent and efficient self with me, though, so I have no reason to believe there was foul play involved.

"Send him in."

Asher walks in a minute later, and my nose wrinkles as I take in his appearance.

"What the fuck are you wearing?" I ask.

He glances down at his clothes. "You don't like the fit?"

"The fit?" I repeat.

"The outfit," he clarifies.

He's wearing saggy pants, crocs on his feet, and a shirt with flamingoes all over it. One is larger than the rest, zoomed in on its face, and I feel like it's staring at me.

"It's certainly…unique," I say, not one to judge my brother's sense of style. Or lack thereof.

"Did you call me in to criticize my clothing choices today?" he asks.

I clear my throat. "Not at all. Wear what you feel good in. That's what I always say."

"And you feel good in another pair of chinos and an Aces polo shirt?" he presses.

I glance down at my own *fit*. "It's comfortable," I say a little defensively. It's also professional, but I have a feeling the dude in the flamingo shirt won't really care.

"So are the flamings."

"The flamings? Oh, do you mean the *flamingoes*? Are we just…shortening all the words now?"

He sighs. "You're so fucking old, dude."

"Right. Well, anyway. What the fuck was with your false start call yesterday?" I pull up the footage of his penalty and run it on the screens in my office—one behind me so he can see it, the other behind him so I can see it.

His eyes don't watch the screen. Instead, he's looking at me. "Sorry Coach. I'll do better."

"You're damn right you will. It cost us five yards."

"So?" he says a little flippantly, and I can't say I appreciate his *tude* right now.

"So that could've been the difference between winning and losing. We scored a field goal on that try. We might've gotten a touchdown if you hadn't set us back a down. Every yard counts."

GAME PLAY

"Yeah, yeah. It's fucking preseason, man."

My brows shoot up. "You're new to this team," I begin, ready to tell him that the culture here is to play our fucking hardest even when the games don't matter, but he interrupts me.

"So are you," he points out.

His words only serve to pulse my anger. "Correct, but if you want to continue starting for me, you need to do better. Plenty of guys want your spot, and you earned it in camp, but if you don't play like you want to keep it, I'll bench you faster than you can abbreviate another word."

"You know I play better than those guys."

I clench my jaw for a beat. "Maybe you do, maybe you don't. But you're not doing yourself any favors talking back to the coach just because he's your brother. Now get the fuck out of my office, and if you ever talk to me like that again, you'll be running suicides until you vomit. Hear me?"

"Yeah," he mutters, and he stands to leave without another word.

Maybe that wasn't the most motivational meeting I've had with a player, but I can't have him strutting around in his stupid *fits* thinking he has some advantage because I'm his brother. I need to be as hard on him as I am on any other player...if not harder. And suicide drills where he runs from the goal line to the ten-yard line, then back to the goal line and to the twenty, all the way down the field over and over—that's usually the way to get through to just about any player.

So when he gets called for illegal use of hands when he pushes a player before he moves to catch a ball Miles fired at him in the next game, I'm furious. Especially because this time we lose ten yards and we were already on a third down.

The game comes down to a field goal at the wire that goes the way of the Bengals at their home stadium, and I'm fucking livid.

I realize it's a team effort and it never comes down to just one play. Furthermore, I realize that there was more than one penalty in this game despite going over the issues with my players in the last game. There will *always* be penalties. That's just the nature of the game.

Maybe I'm expecting more out of my brother after our talk. Maybe I expected a cleaner game because I came down hard on him.

Maybe he needs to run a few suicides as penance for his penalty.

We get in late on Sunday night, but I still call him in Monday morning at nine. He's wearing another ridiculous outfit, and his eyes won't meet mine as I basically blame him for losing the game for us.

I'm in a bad mood the rest of the day as I meet with every player who committed a penalty during the game, but Tuesdays are our day off, and I text Jolene just as I'm leaving the office.

Me: *Any chance I can see you tonight?*

Her response is quick.

Lorraine: *Is this a booty call, a dinner date, or an overnight?*

My chest tightens as I think about what I need, and I know what I need is a good night of sleep holding her in my arms.

Me: *All of the above if possible.*

Lorraine: *I'll see what I can swing.*

Me: *I miss you.*

Lorraine: *[teary eye emoji] I miss you, too.*

GAME PLAY

As it turns out, she can swing coming over at nine, which is just after Jonah goes to sleep. The boys are back in school now, and Jolene said Sam was fine with getting both boys off to school in the morning.

The moment she appears at my front door, I pull her into my arms. I let out a heavy breath that feels like I've been holding onto since the last time I got to hold her in my arms like this. Every time I've seen her since our first preseason game, our time together has been rushed.

I don't want to rush.

I just want *time* with her.

I kiss her and pull her inside, slamming the door shut behind her.

"What's going on?" she asks breathlessly.

"Nothing. Just been a tough couple weeks and I guess I needed this more than I realized."

"So did I," she admits, clinging to me just as I am to her as she nestles into my chest.

We stand there quietly, just holding one another as we practice deep breathing exercises, and I feel instantly calm having her here in my arms.

"Can I get you some wine?" I finally ask, and she nods against my chest.

"I'd love some. I'll take my bag upstairs and meet you in the kitchen in three minutes."

"Deal," I say, and I press my lips softly to hers as she heads upstairs to my bedroom—a room that feels like *our* bedroom when she's here.

I pour a rather large tumbler of whiskey for myself and a glass of wine for her, and it's probably only been about ninety seconds when I hear the doorbell ring.

"Fuck," I mutter, and I head over to the door to get rid of whoever is visiting me at this late hour when all I want is some time alone with Jolene.

I see my brother standing on my porch when I glance through the peephole, and I open the door.

He's wearing normal clothes this time, which tells me he's been wearing those dumb outfits to purposely irk me, but the expression on his face is not normal at all.

"Is Sam here?" he demands when he walks past me as I hold the door open.

I shake my head. Maybe he saw her car out on the street in front of the house and that's why he asked, but I can't tell him who really *is* here. He didn't ask, though. He asked specifically about Sam.

"Good," he says. "Because I need your help. I'm in a lot of trouble."

I'm about to warn him that we aren't alone before he starts talking, but he plows forward.

And the very last thing I need is someone from the media overhearing his next words.

CHAPTER 33

Jolene

"I need your help. I'm in a lot of trouble." I hear Asher's voice, and clearly he thinks Lincoln is alone and he's confessing something to his brother who just happens to be his head coach.

I don't want to listen to them. It's a private conversation not meant for me, and certainly not meant for a reporter, so I step back into Lincoln's room even though Asher's voice carries up the hallway.

And I hear everything he says next.

"I'm in deep with some bookies. I need money, and I don't know where else to turn."

Holy shit.

My eyes widen at his confession as my stomach twists.

"What were you betting on?" Lincoln demands.

Asher clears his throat loudly. "Games. I made a shit load when we won, but I bet on the second game and we lost, and, well...here I am."

"What the fuck, man?" Lincoln practically roars.

Oh my God. I should *not* be overhearing this. What do I do?

I panic, and I freeze.

I can't know this stuff. I'm with the media, and I promised Marcus when I confessed that Lincoln and I have a secret relationship that I would report fairly and honestly, and now this breaking story falls right into my lap?

I can't report on this. I can't. It would only worsen the feud between our families and put both Asher's and Lincoln's careers in jeopardy, and I won't do that.

Besides, Lincoln will do the right thing. He has to. I realize it's his brother, but it's also his team at stake here. It's his responsibility to report player misconduct, and I just don't see him as the guy who sweeps these things under the rug.

"Listen to me, Asher," I hear Lincoln say. He lowers his voice, and I can't make out his next words.

I draw in a deep breath and slowly exhale, and I wait upstairs until I hear the front door open and close again.

"Who was that?" I ask brightly when I walk down the stairs, and I know it's *too* bright considering what just happened, but I'm not that good of an actress.

"A player," he grunts, and he really thinks I didn't hear a thing.

I feel a twist in my back that he didn't tell me the truth—or, at the very least, that he's lying by omission.

"Ready for that glass of wine?" he asks, and I nod. "Start without me. I have to take care of something. I'll be right back." He disappears down the hall toward his office, and I hear the door click shut as I head into the kitchen to wait for him.

He returns when my glass is almost empty, and it's not because I've been chugging it.

GAME PLAY

"Sorry. That took longer than I expected." He must've called Jack to tell him what's going on, and I feel a sense of relief that he did the right thing.

I still don't admit I heard everything, though.

He picks up his tumbler and drains the whiskey in it in a few gulps.

"I'm exhausted. You ready to go to sleep?" he asks.

I abandon my wine and follow him upstairs. He takes a quick shower and meets me in bed, and then he flicks off the light without much more than a quick kiss and a muttered goodnight, and I'm left to wonder why he even invited me here in the first place tonight.

I spend the night chewing over the information I know that he's not sharing with me, and I hardly sleep at all because of it.

There's enough between us already. We don't need yet another mountain to climb or another earthquake to widen the chasm. Yet I already feel it happening.

When morning dawns and his alarm goes off, I'm awake—already or still, I'm not sure. I wait for him to make the first move, and he does. He sighs, shuts off his alarm, and gets out of bed without a word, without a kiss or a hug or a touch.

Disappointment fills me. He's going to let it come between us, and maybe this is when I should admit I heard everything.

I hear his shower turn on, and I debate what to do.

I should head home, or join him in the shower, but I feel like I'm in a haze and I don't know how to handle it.

I've been lying in bed with my promise to Marcus running through my head. When he asked me what I'd do if I ran into something Lincoln wouldn't want public, I made a promise.

If it needs to be made public, I assure you, it will be.

This doesn't *need* to be made public. But is ignoring the fact that I know sweeping a big problem under the rug? In particular when I know that *Lincoln* knows and he might not be doing anything about it?

It's a bad position to be in, and I think not for the first time that maybe Rivera would've been better suited to this position.

I earned it, though, and I will figure out what to do with what I know.

A text comes through from Marcus while I try to piece everything together, and his words only further press my guilt into my chest.

Marcus: *Mom is doing well. She'll be in the hospital another few days and then we can work on getting her moved. Thanks for all your hard work at the office. I'll be out another two weeks or so but I'm glad to know you and Rivera are playing nice.*

I'm in the process of drafting a reply when another text comes through. This one, however, is from the devil himself, Ryan Rivera.

Rivera: *Another two weeks with me in charge. I'm guessing you don't want the scandal that would come with publishing these photos, right? You should really be more careful.*

He sends a handful of photos from last night. They show me getting into Sam's car. In my haste to get to Lincoln, I guess I forgot to pull up my hood.

The next one shows me getting out at Lincoln's place and slinging my duffel over my shoulder. Another shows me walking up to the door, and the final two show him greeting

GAME PLAY

me last night when he hauled me into his arms and kissed me the moment the door opened.

Another text comes through as I study the last two photos.

It's clear to see it's me with Lincoln. There must be some telephoto lens in use, and my stomach twists at the thought that he's been having me followed just so he could catch me doing something wrong.

Rivera: *Unless you want a scandal on your hands, you need to resign your position as team correspondent.*

I flip through the photos again.

As far as anyone knows, Lincoln is dating my best friend...yet I'm showing up on his doorstep and kissing him late at night.

Not only would this make *me* look like a homewrecker, thus killing my credibility with my viewers, but it would confirm the accusations that Lincoln is a cheater, *and* it would reveal our secret relationship to both our families...and on top of that, I promised to report with honesty and integrity, and now I'm holding onto this massive secret that could put not one but *two* of Eddie Nash's sons' careers in jeopardy if anyone ever found out, further deepening the divide between our families all because of me.

I can't let Rivera break this scandal. I don't want to lose my job, but I have to protect Lincoln. I have to protect *myself*. I have to protect our families.

It looks like I'm out of options.

TO BE CONTINUED IN BOOK 4, OVERTIME

Our secret relationship is revealed when a devious colleague who wants my job decides to print the undercover photos that he took of us. But he doesn't just call us out for getting together on the sly. Instead, he insinuates that Lincoln is a cheater while damaging my own reputation, too.

My job is on the line, my family won't talk to me, and it feels like my life is falling apart. I hold onto Lincoln as the chaos swirls around us with the inevitable end always in sight.

It feels like we're in overtime and we're about to lose everything.

Acknowledgments

I'll save my acknowledgments for the final book! I can't wait for you to see what's coming next...

xoxo,
Lisa Suzanne

About the Author

Lisa Suzanne is a romance author who resides in Arizona with her husband and two kids. She's a former high school English teacher and college composition instructor. When she's not chasing or cuddling her kids, she can be found working on her latest book or watching reruns of *Friends*.

Also by Lisa Suzanne

HOME GAME

Vegas Aces Book One
#1 Bestselling Sports Romance

CURVEBALL

Vegas Heat: The Expansion Team
Book One

Made in United States
North Haven, CT
12 September 2024